once

s*h*e

dreamed

ABBI GLINES

for Jack Britton Sullivan

You came into my life when I was sure I didn't need anyone. Especially a man. You showed me I did need someone, but someone who would let me, be me. Thank you.

once
she
dreamed

One

"**E**GGS DON'T GATHER themselves," were the familiar words my momma called out at five a.m. this morning, as she swung open our bedroom door. I shared a room with my three sisters. Always had. We lived in a house with only five rooms, two of those being for beds.

Yawning I wondered if I'd ever get to sleep late. Just one day in my life have a chance to sleep past seven. Oh, what a treat that would be.

"Stop daydreaming and go get the eggs. Sammy Jo, did you hear me? Momma will go to hollering in a few minutes if they're not in the kitchen. Do I got to do everythin' around here?" Milly was the oldest of the four of us. She just turned nineteen this past September. We thought she might get married to that Garner boy but he ran off to join the Marines. No one expected that. Especially Milly, didn't see it coming. However, I think momma was more let down than Milly. She was hoping for one less mouth to feed.

"Are you listening?" she yelled at me this time.

Sighing, I covered yet another yawn and glared at Milly above me. She acted bossy, but truth of it is, I'm only eleven months younger than her. I would turn nineteen this August. "I hear you. Jesus, stop with the yapping," I grumbled and lightly coughed.

Hazel giggled behind me. I turned my head to wink at my sister. At only ten years old Hazel was the youngest and I thought she'd be the baby forever, daddy having passed on from skin cancer, which seemed to freeze her in time. Make Hazel forever the baby. Then three years ago momma hooked up with a man traveling through town and all he left her was a swollen tummy. Now, none of us wish it any different. Henry is adored by the lot of us.

"I'm not milking the damn cow again," Bessy said, stomping her feet, putting both her hands on her hips with all of Bessy's dramatic flair. "I did it last week. It's someone else's turn." Bessy was fifteen and exhausting. I really hoped she ended up on a stage. She would be a superstar with all that drama that comes so natural to her.

"You're scared of the chickens," Milly reminded her. "Milk the cow or go feed the hogs. You said they stunk last week. Make up your mind and stop cussing like a man."

I finished gathering the eggs and headed for the house. Those two would bicker over cows for several more minutes at least. When momma yelled I didn't want trouble. I had plans tonight and I needed her in a mood, the best one currently possible.

"Come back and help little Diva with the milking," Milly called out after me.

I ignored her. She wasn't my boss.

Opening the screen door I stepped into the kitchen. Momma's back was to me as she cut the shortening and butter into the flour for biscuits. "Want me to put the pot roast in the slow cooker?" I asked trying to be helpful. Overly helpful mind you.

"I reckon we need to do that. Vilma didn't say how old it was so I don't want a roast going bad. Was nice of her to bring it over like that. Something to say for good neighbors."

Maybe so, good neighbors, but this here town was not my idea of a life. I wanted out of Moulton. Out of Alabama. Anywhere but here. There was a big ol' world waiting to meet me and my dream was to see it all. Or as much as I could in a life.

I pulled my pale blonde hair into the rubber band I kept on my wrist as a habit. The morning breeze had tangled my hair. I didn't care, I was low maintenance, I'd brush the wads out later. I had some sucking up to my momma to do to convince her to let me go with Jamie and Ben to a concert. Tonight in Cullman, Alabama was *Rock the South* and they had an extra ticket. I'd never been to a concert before.

"Momma, what time do you have to go to work?" I asked, pulling out the slow cooker, looking for things to be done, though I'm a worker and she expects this.

"Need to be at the bakery by eight. Sara got there at five this morning to start the morning pastries. I'm on cupcakes and cookies today. Thought I'd try a new banana bread too. Those always sell good, no matter."

Momma had been working for Sweethouse Bakery for over twelve years this month. Some weeks she did the morning shift and we were left with Milly to wake us. Those days were not my favorite.

"You're working the front counter from nine to four. Be early Sammy Jo. I left a list of things for Bessy and Hazel to do around the house. Bessy needs to keep an eye on the roast. The list is there on the table."

"Yes ma'am," I replied, walking over to the table, jotting down Bessy's chore.

While I worked with momma at the bakery, Milly went to cosmetology school. She passed her exams and had a new job at the only hair salon in town, the one and only to ever exist. She didn't have to go to work until ten every morning but she often worked till seven. Sometimes worked right past it. I had no idea there were so many heads to cut and groom and style. There were barely over three thousand residents in Moulton, Alabama proper. How a hair salon could stay that busy was beyond my imagination. Where were these folks going? The bakery sat close enough to the main road headed from Cullman to Florence. That gave it commuter traffic. But a hair salon in Moulton, Alabama seemed plain silly to me. All folks do is stare at each other, in the street, at church or home. If they were bald, they'd do the same thing.

"Momma! Momma! I lost my fwog!" Henry called to her as he burst through the door with dirt smeared on his face already, his bottom lip pooched and trembling.

"Go wash up and get ready for breakfast. More frogs where he came from. You can catch one later." Her response was unconcerned. I made a mental note to help Henry find a frog after breakfast, if not sooner.

His bottom lip stayed pooched as he nodded his head then walked back to the bathroom. Momma had never babied him, but he sure got enough from his sisters.

"Is Bessy and Hazel watching Henry today or is he going to the bakery with us?" I asked chopping up the celery to add to the roast, taking a nibble now and then.

"Bessy can watch him. He hates being there. Says the women pinch at his cheeks. Makes 'em eat up all the profits."

He ate his weight in cookies and momma hated that. But there was nothing much for Henry to do at the bakery where Henry had actually been born. Momma hadn't been able to take days off at the end of her pregnancy then. We flat needed the money to eat. Milly and I had been working after school to help but it wasn't enough. When momma's water broke there had been no time to get her to Cullman to the hospital. Henry was born on the tile floor with the help of Sara and Vilma.

I felt bad for momma. The whole situation. She had a baby with her babies around her, no father there to help. After losing my daddy I didn't figure a man could live up to his memory. But still . . . I wondered if momma had been scared. She sure didn't seem to be.

That day I made a promise to myself. I wouldn't have a baby on the floor of a bakery without its daddy around. I'd marry a man who loved me and could give me the world in pieces. When our baby was born he'd be holding my hand safely nestled somewhere else, likely in a hospital in New York City, Chicago, Boston, or maybe Seattle, anywhere but here.

Two

THE SMELL OF strawberry cupcakes filled the air of the bakery making my stomach rumble. I longed, but could not taste. Momma would slap my hand. She could tell when I wanted to touch one. Inside the cake were fresh strawberries and the icing was made with cream cheese. Homemade, not from the carton. I'd watched momma make them many times. I always wanted to lick the spoon, but never got the chance.

It was after two and I hadn't got the nerve to ask momma if I could go to the concert. I kept waiting to catch her when she wasn't so busy, but she'd been working most of the day, sweating and straining in the kitchen, skipping lunch to stay ahead. There hadn't been a good time to ask her. Momma could not stop.

The bell above the door chimed, snapping me out of my cupcake gaze. I quickly stood up from my stool and got my smile in the greeting position. My breath caught just a little as I took in the man in front of me. He was tall and also beautiful, and he dressed and smelled expensive. I could smell his expensiveness over the cupcakes and that was saying a lot. Men like him didn't walk into here, not a bakery in Moulton, Alabama.

"Hello," I said cheerily. "We have fresh strawberry cupcakes that just came out of the oven. There's also warm apple tarts and blueberry muffins with blueberries that came off the farm, straight outta Mable Richards' field." Although I normally told everyone who walked in the bakery what we had available, I felt silly saying it to him. He didn't seem like the kind to eat any of that stuff. I'd imagined he drank champagne, ate caviar, or something like that.

"Oh, and we have banana nut bread. It's new and I haven't had any, but my momma never makes anything from scratch that ain't just perfectly delicious." I had to add that and sound even sillier. And that was pretty silly.

His gaze stopped scanning the small tiny bakery and then it locked on me. His eyes were green. Around them clear white. Not the dark green that almost looks brown, but light green, like light on grass. The kind that makes you want to stare right at them, while they're staring right at you. For a long long time, or forever and ever, either one was fine.

"What do you suggest?" When his deep voice asked it was thick like the whiskey I'd tried with Ben that time. He'd snuck it out of his dad's private stash.

"Huh?" That was all that came out of my mouth. That man's voice was intoxicating. He even sounded expensive I tell you. I hadn't known people could sound expensive. Like he had gold in his stomach or something.

A grin tugged at his lips and I caught myself smiling back at him. I bet his full smile was something else. "What item do you suggest I try?" He repeated himself and oh, the man was trying to order. I shook my head to clear it then glanced down at the cupcakes waiting there. "The strawberry cupcakes are delicious. I mean, uh, I think they are. They smell so good and have fresh strawberries and I imagine they taste real nice."

"I'll take three," he replied.

I beamed. He was going to love them. "Okay," I said, reaching for a box before slipping on the plastic gloves. We had to wear them when touching the food.

"Do you serve coffee?" he asked.

I nodded. "Oh yes! We have a fresh pot on. I'll get you a large if you like?"

"Thank you," he responded.

I wanted to look back at him, but I kept my attention on my task, tried not to drop anything. "Does your momma own the place?" His voice interrupted my concentration and I almost dropped the cupcakes.

"My momma?" I repeated then laughed a little. "No, my momma just works here. Sure wish she could own a place like this. She'd be real good at it."

I placed his box of cupcakes on the counter then put his coffee right beside it. "That'll be seven dollars and fifty-two cents." I folded napkins on top of the box and goofily smiled with embarrassment.

From a fist-sized wad he pulled a ten-dollar bill and handed it across the counter. "Keep the change," he said.

That was two dollars and forty-eight cents he was leaving behind for a tip. Why in the world would he do that? I started to speak when he opened the box and withdrew a fresh baked cupcake. The smell hit my nose and I inhaled deeply, he taking a napkin and his coffee in hand and he was ready to test my opinion.

"If it's as good as you say it is, I'm sure I'll be right back." He then turned to leave kind of slowly. His box with the other two cupcakes sat on the counter as placed. I picked them up and then called out. "You're forgetting your other cupcakes!"

He stopped at the door and turned back to me grinning. A real smile crept across his face. "I bought those for you," he replied. Then he left. Just like that. Walked away before I could even say thank you.

I looked down at the cupcakes and my mouth began to water, but I wouldn't eat them both. I'd take one home for Henry. Momma may not be thrilled about it, but the man bought the cupcakes for me. I didn't ask him to and Henry would love it and that's all I needed to know.

Opening the box back up I lifted a cupcake out. Then I took my very first bite. It melted on my tongue like sugar. My toes curled in my shoes.

"Sammy Jo what are you doing!" My momma's voice startled me to shaking. When I opened my eyes to see her, she was glaring at me with that special momma stare, like a naughty child had been caught.

"It's mine," I replied, my mouth still full of the yummy goodness I was holding. "A man just bought three and left me two." I finished chewing wishing I could savor the taste left in my mouth.

"A man did what?" she asked, her hands on her hips as she huffed.

"A man," I said pointing at the door. "He was just in here, just now. He asked me what I'd buy if it were up to me and I told him the strawberry cupcakes. So he then bought three with a coffee. He took one out, said the others were for me, and walked right out the door."

Momma sighed and shook her head then mumbled something. She wasn't happy, but I was eating my cupcake, so I was having a hard time caring.

"I won't eat both. I'm taking Henry the other." I figured mentioning Henry would soften her up. It didn't soften her any.

"You shouldn't allow strange men to buy you things. Men only buy women gifts, because they're after sex and the way you look" -she shook her finger at me and frowned- "you can see in a mirror just fine. The Lord decided to give you all them looks and men notice them for what they want. Ain't got nothing to do with you. And you got to be careful about it."

I had heard this lecture before. About men wanting me and me needing to protect myself from the predators about. Daddy had warned me when I started junior high. He said, "you're too pretty for your own damn good and I'd hate to have to shoot some boy, for forgettin' you're my child."

"He walked out before I could stop him. Momma, he was rich. He even smelled expensive. He won't be coming back around here. People here don't look like him."

Momma frowned and stared at the door. "He'll be back. He got a look at you. That's all it takes to return." She then turned and headed back to the kitchen.

I wasn't sure how I felt about my very own momma thinking men all wanted me. I didn't particularly believe I was really that attractive, especially to a man like that one.

Three

I KNEW AFTER the cupcake incident momma would say no to the concert. But I'd held out hope and asked anyway and yep, she said no. She needed me home for shelling picked peas and canning them after that. In June parts of the garden were ready and each month we had things to put up. We ate from our garden all winter. Next month would be tomatoes and I hated canning them. But I also hated shelling peas.

Milly had been asked on a date. Robbie Long was his name and since momma was hoping to marry her off real soon, she let her go hoping he would ask. The rest of us were sitting under the oak shelling peas and chatting amongst us. Even Henry was shelling away.

Technically, Ben had been a date. Sure we had been friends forever and we weren't about to get married, but still, it seemed unfair. I couldn't date at all. Instead my fingers were getting raw from the hulls and we still had several more steps to go before we could sleep.

I had to admit, if telling the truth, that the cupcake was

completely worth it. Henry agreed with that. Most of the icing ended up on his face, which made him even cuter. As if that was possible to do.

"Tell me about the cupcake man. Again, tell it once more." Bessy was starry eyed about the whole idea. You might say slightly possessed.

"Nothing to tell," momma replied, with a grumble and a snap of her fingers.

Bessy looked disappointed. She knew not to push momma when she sounded like that. I knew the same so I didn't.

"I want annuder cupcate," Henry said, smiling at the last of his words.

"On your birthday," momma replied.

That sent him into singing the happy birthday song and he sang it and sang it and sang it.

"When do I get to work at the bakery?" Bessy asked and Bessy knew the answer. She wouldn't get to work there anytime soon. Momma needed her to watch little Henry during the summer months. I didn't say that to her. She hadn't been asking me.

"When Sammy Jo marries and moves on," was momma's quick reply.

Visions of me marrying a man and "moving on" danced in my head and I smiled. That was my favorite daydream. Problem was no one around here was going to sweep me off my feet. Or take me out of this town. They'd all die here in Moulton. Spend their lives barely leaving and their lives would be done. I was headed in that direction.

"She's picky. Lots of guys ask her out but Sammy Jo never goes," Bessy said, frowning at me. "She's the prettiest girl in this town but she never dates any boys."

I had heard this before and I was tiring of defending myself on the subject.

"No guy in this town can get me away. I want to see the world. I don't want to set up house in Moulton and spit out babies till I'm old."

Bessy rolled her eyes. "Ain't nothing wrong with that. Your looks got you all high falutin'. You think you deserve more than me and it ain't fair you know. If I'd been born with your blonde hair, big boobs and dancer's legs, I'd have me a man already with a house all to myself."

I wanted Bessy to dream bigger than that, but like Milly that wasn't possible.

"I don't just want a man. I want an epic romance."

Bessy laughed and tossed an empty shell into the trash with disgust. "You've been reading too many books."

"That's enough," momma said. "I'm tired of hearing this." She handed me a gallon sized bucket of peas already shelled. "Go on inside with these. Vilma lent me her fancy pressure canner. Said it's safer to use than the old one. Go figure it out. Get it going. She left directions beside it."

This was momma's way to get rid of me. She wanted quiet on the subject of marriage. Not once had she ever corrected me for wanting out of here. She seemed to agree with me. And I think she believed I'd achieve it. I would. Yes, I would.

"Me ont to go too," Henry said, running toward me and smiling.

"That's fine. Stay away from the canning. You could get hurt," momma told him.

I returned little Henry's grin. "I'll let you help me fill the jars with peas."

He clapped like that was exciting and I guess to him it was. Funny thing was I hated peas. Every jar we canned meant I'd have to eat them at some point along the way. I'd much rather be canning fruit. Or making strawberry preserves. Then I could appreciate the hard work.

When I stepped inside the phone was ringing. I sat the pot of peas on the table and hurried to pick it up.

"Hello"

"Hey, Sam, Jamie said you couldn't go tonight. Thought I'd call and see if I could change your mind. I got that ticket for you. Hate to give it to someone else."

Ben was the sweetest guy I knew. He had moved to Moulton to live with his dad when he was in the fourth grade. Jamie and I had been best friends since kindergarten. We saw the shy little boy with glasses and I pulled him into our pack. The three of us had been close ever since.

Except sometimes I felt like Ben might want more than that. At least lately I felt that way. He treated me different than Jamie. She had brought it up a few times and I had tried to change the subject. But she wasn't the only one picking that up. Ben was definitely acting interested. Like he had a spotlight on me.

"Momma has us canning peas tonight. You know how much I love that." I added sarcasm to my voice so he would understand that I had really wanted to go with them.

"That sucks. You don't think I could talk her into letting you go?" he asked with hope in his tone.

If I tried to get momma in here to chat she might put me in the pressure canner. "Uh, no. She already has me inside starting the canning process. Milly May is on a date and that's the only child momma can spare tonight. She needs me here. I really wanted to go. Thank you for the invite."

Maybe it was best that I wasn't going. I didn't want Ben to get the wrong idea. He'd always just be my friend. One of my best friends ever and there's something to say for that.

"Yeah, okay. I understand. Jerry's wanting to go so he can have your ticket. I'll miss you though, I will."

Not a "we will miss you," but an "I will miss you." Yikes . . . I had to get us back to the way we were. Maybe I could fix Ben up with a girl in town or something like that?

"That's a good idea. Jerry will love it. Y'all have fun," I told him.

"Bye, Sam." His voice held a touch of sadness. Me not going was that sadness in his voice. That frightened and scared me I tell you.

"Bye," I replied, then quickly hung up. I had to talk to Jamie about this. We needed to fix Ben up with someone else and fast. I didn't want to lose a friendship because Ben might think there was more to us in the future. He was my buddy. He needed to remember that. Ben was Moulton. He'd never leave. I had dreams. And they weren't in this town.

Four

I HADN'T EXPECTED to see Ben and Jamie walking in the door of the bakery the next morning. Although it was almost lunchtime it was still early for them. I was sure their night had been a late one. I wanted to hear what had happened, but not with momma around.

"Hey y'all," I said, happy to see them.

Jamie immediately chimed in about the smell: "God it smells like heaven in here. I'd weigh two hundred pounds if I worked here. I struggle enough as it is. How you work in this bakery and don't get fat is unfair you precious thing." Jamie always fussed about her weight. She wasn't fat, Jamie was curvy. She always battled to shed fifteen pounds but I thought she was fine like she was.

"If you had my momma you'd not gain weight," I whispered, cupping my hand over my mouth.

Ben frowned and looked at the lemon cupcakes alongside the blueberry muffins. Beside them were the apple tarts. "Shame she won't let you eat that."

"No it's not. It's a gift from God. She'd be fat if she could,"

Jamie argued, slapping his arm in a way that seemed less friendly, more "look at me," which was interesting and intriguing I admit.

"Sam doesn't eat enough to get fat. And she hardly ever sits still." Ben argued as if he were defending my weight. Then his eyes shot across me really fast. Like a shadow or a beam from the sun, as if to see if I'd really heard him.

Jamie rolled her eyes, but she seemed a little hurt, annoyed you might say. Maybe I was reading too much into this though there was something in her gestures. Something Ben was missing . . . and I had also missed it apparently.

"One day I'll bake my own cupcakes. Eat 'em until I'm so fat I waddle and then tump over." I teased, wanting to lighten the mood, because I had to change the tenseness.

Jamie laughed: "sure you will. You'll marry some guy from another state and run off to see the world. You have the looks, just need Mr. Wonderful to discover you hereabouts." She sighed and looked around the bakery. "Not sure he'll find you here."

"Why would she move to another state?" Ben asked and seemed annoyed.

"Because she's been talking about it since she was five years old. She doesn't want to live in a two-story house in the middle of Moulton, Alabama, with five kids and a farmer for a husband. She wants an adventure. Listen to her!" Jamie knew me well. We had stretched ourselves on the steep grassy hill behind my house on many summer days discussing our dreams and wants. We were girls wanting to be women, forgetting that the now was simpler, when later it wouldn't be. Jamie's dream was exactly what she'd just said she didn't want for me. I wondered if Ben knew that.

"Nothing wrong with Alabama or Moulton," Ben replied, sounding defensive.

"Ben, it's not what I want for me. But for others it's perfectly fine. Now, as much as I'd love the play by play of last night I can't do that. Momma will come out from the kitchen and skin my hide if I chat."

"Don't you get a lunch break?" Ben asked.

Jamie, however, laughed at his question. "Seriously, I'd swear you'd never in your life met her momma if I didn't know better. Marjaline Knox ain't letting her off for lunch or to pee."

Jamie was right. Momma would bring me a tuna salad sandwich, or something of that nature at noon. I'd have to eat it sitting right here. There were no other employees to take my place so I couldn't step outside.

"Well, could you at least go out after work? Get an ice cream or something like that? Jerry said a bunch were swimming at the lake. We could go meet up with them."

Since momma told me no last night there was a chance she'd let me go. "I'll ask. I probably can. Y'all come by at four to check. Bring me a suit just in case?" I asked Jamie, more of a telling, because I knew I had a suit at her house.

The door chimed and Jamie took Ben's arm to move him away from the counter.

"Afternoon kids," Mrs. Peabody said as she shuffled inside the bakery. Her white hair was neatly fashioned on top of her head. The yellow sunflower-dress her staple. What the lady was known to wear. I'd seen it enough to remember. "Marjaline made any of that blueberry cobbler? Elroy was a fan of that. Thought I might get him some. Not that neither of us needs it."

"No ma'am, not today. We have apple tarts. But if momma has the ingredients she could probably make you one. You could pick it up later in the day."

Enthusiastically she nodded her head. "That would be just perfect. Elroy's been out working the fields and he needs him a tooth-rottin' sweet treat. I'm making some homemade vanilla ice cream and that cobbler would do the trick."

"Let me go ask her," I said. With a smile I glanced at my friends who were waiting quietly at a distance. I wished they'd leave in case momma came out. She didn't like me visiting with friends, not during my shift anyway. But I couldn't tell them to leave without sounding rude or haughty. They had placed me in an uncomfortable spot.

I hurried back to the kitchen, which wasn't really far, just as momma was retrieving several hot loaves of cinnamon raisin bread. I hoped she'd take home a loaf for us. Hazel loved that stuff.

"Momma, Mrs Peabody is here and she's wanting a blueberry cobbler. Said Mr. Peabody loved the last one and she wanted to get him a sweet treat. Reckon you can make her one? She'll come back later and get it."

Momma put the loaves down and waited. She glanced around and then at me. "I got what I need, I think. Them blueberry's need to be used. Tell her it'll be ready at three."

Momma liked making a sell. But more than that she liked people wanting her food. It made her feel special and needed. My momma could bake better than the best, countywide and everyone knew it. I wished she had a place of her own. She ran the bakery like it was. Why wouldn't her own be successful?

"She'll be tickled pink," I said. I then turned to hurry back to the store front hoping momma wouldn't follow.

"She said she'd have you one by three. Nice and fresh from the oven."

Mrs. Peabody clapped her hands. Her smile covered her face. "She's a good one, that Marjaline, the solidest God ever made!"

I agreed. I really did. She was strict but the woman was precious.

Mrs. Peabody nodded to Jamie and Ben then waved to me as she left. "I'll be back through around three. Thank you sweetie," she said.

When the door closed behind her Jamie giggled. "Never seen a woman so happy about a cobbler."

I shrugged and then I informed her: "you ain't had my momma's cobbler."

Five

B EN PULLED HIS old Ford truck onto the grassy hill by the lake. It had belonged to his grandfather for ten more years than Ben had been on the planet. Momma agreed to let me go as long as I was home by seven thirty to wash the supper dishes. That gave me three hours to swim and hang out with my friends.

The few that had been lucky enough to go off to college were all back for the summer. The rest of us were here working and a couple were actually getting married and starting their life in Moulton. Here, in hell, forever.

Jamie wanted that life. So I tried never to talk about how that was my biggest nightmare. It was her dream and I didn't want to belittle that. Even if I couldn't understand it, her dreams were hers to have.

We dropped our towels down on a clear spot and I scanned the crowd to see Marilyn Marcus tangled around Jack Harold. The ring on her hand was small, but the stone still caught the sunlight. She'd been in the bakery just last week announcing her engagement and wanting to talk to momma about making her cake. It had taken all my acting abilities to smile and pretend like what she was saying was wonderful news to me. Deep down all I could remember was that time in eighth grade when we were supposed to write down where we saw ourselves in ten years and only Marilyn and I had written down that we saw ourselves somewhere fabulous and away from Alabama. Now she was marrying a farmer's son. Not that it was a bad thing. It was just that she wasn't getting out. She wouldn't walk the streets of Manhattan, or go to cocktail parties with her dream guy, her millionaire fiancé.

Don't get me wrong. I wasn't holding on for a rich man to get me out of Moulton. I simply wanted an adventure. Let me see the world. Anything but what Marilyn was facing.

"Can you believe she's engaged," Jamie said, coming up beside me. She must have caught me looking their way. "I thought for sure she'd run off. Get out of town. Now that ain't gonna happen."

Me too. But I didn't say that.

"Guess when you love someone, where they are is where you'll be." Ben spoke, causing us both to turn to look at him. His gaze was on mine and it felt like he was saying something I didn't want to hear. I flashed a smile and shook my head. "Guess I better not fall in love unless he lives in Chicago or New York City, maybe Seattle or Boston."

Jamie laughed. I grinned at her.

"I don't imagine you ever in love. Sammy Jo Knox in love?" Jamie said it and I knew that she meant it. I had never had crushes on a boy. Because the boys here were just that, they were here where I didn't want to be.

"Maybe I won't. Maybe I'll conquer the world single and enjoy every minute of doing it."

Jamie linked her arm with mine. "I hope you do Sam. I really do."

I would. That was something I was sure of. I just wasn't sure how at the moment.

"Heard Milly May and Richard were tight as ticks last night at the movies. Rumor has it they left early and went parking. Wonder if she'll be wearing a ring. Reckon she will really soon."

My stomach felt sick. I knew that's what my sister wanted, but was afraid she wanted it so badly she'd settle for whoever would give it. This wasn't nineteen fifty anymore. A woman didn't have to get married by the age of twenty. Jesus, what was everyone's problem?

"Your momma hoping she gets married soon?" Jamie asked. I told her the truth. Momma wanted to marry her off and then I'd be next in the raffle. If only we'd been a bunch of boys. She'd have less to worry about. No one rushed sons into marriage. They kept them around as long as they could to cherish their independence.

"Enough marriage talk. Let's go swim," Ben said, reaching for my arm. Not Jamie's arm, but mine.

"I'll let you swing on the rope first," he said. I glanced back at Jamie as he pulled me away. The hurt look in her eyes told me more than she could or would ever attempt to say. Jamie wanted Ben and that was just another reason I needed out of this town.

As I ran behind Ben to keep from falling down several people called my name. I waved and they waved back. They all got together every day after work. I wasn't as social as them. Momma wouldn't allow it. She knew there wasn't much in Moulton I wanted except my family and the time that I'd served, which was often like a prison sentence.

"You coming to the barn dance Friday?" Drake Red yelled at me. I had forgotten about the dance entirely. It came in mid June then on July the fourth was The Fourth, an even bigger event. I hadn't given any thought to either. I rarely did. Didn't really care.

"Don't know," I called back.

"Go with me," he said with a grin I was sure he thought was sexy. Truth was Drake was handsome. He had the chiseled chest and arms of a worker. And thanks to swimming at the lake he was nice and tan and pretty. His blue eyes had always been a hit with the girls in Moulton, Alabama. Problem was he had no interest in leaving for more than a weekend. He didn't even go to college. He just started working on his daddy's cattle farm and that was where he'd die.

"She's going with me," Ben told him. With that I stopped running and pulled my arm free. Ben had just stepped over the line.

I forgot about Drake and anyone else who might be listening in. I focused on Ben who had stopped in his tracks and was looking at me intensely.

"Why would you say that?" I asked him, not trying to hide my frustration, which was bordering on outright anger.

"I figured if you went, you'd go with me. I was going to ask. I swear it."

I stared without losing control. Did he seriously just say what I think he said as if it were understood? I had never given Ben encouragement. Finally I let out a sigh. "Ben, I don't know what you're thinking or why you'd say something like that. You've been my friend since we were ten. And that's all you'll ever be. I don't want to go to a barn dance with any guy from Moulton or near it. My future isn't here."

I didn't wait for him to say anything more. I turned and came face to face, with Jamie standing like a statue, she looking at me like she was ready to cry and throw herself in attack. This wasn't easy on her. She wanted Ben. But she loved me all the same. She was worried and confused, who isn't. Being young is figuring it out. And it's hard to know what to do.

"Y'all go on and swim. I'm gonna walk home. I need the fresh air and some alone time." I walked away leaving them there. I could feel their eyes on my back and it seemed as if the place had gone silent. I was their drama for the week I guess. Gave them something to talk about.

I should have just gone home after work.

Six

OR THE NEXT two days I didn't hear from Jamie or Ben. I worked then went home and we finished the peas and planted the tomatoes as planned. My regular summer routine, repeated year after year, nothing special and still no hope in sight of escaping this town or state. Milly went on another date with Richard. I might be here forever.

Today was chocolate day. There were chocolate covered strawberries and raspberry cupcakes also stuffed with chocolate. Momma did a chocolate day every week and other than strawberry cupcakes this was my second favorite day. I loved the smell filling the bakery. Those strawberries weren't cheap so I couldn't sneak one, but I sure did swoon and let my mouth water thinking about the sweet tangy juice, the milk chocolate momma made from scratch. She said Marilyn had requested them on her own wedding cake. That would be the tastiest wedding cake on earth ever consumed. I looked forward to that wedding (can't believe I just said that) because I could have my pick of the strawberries. Maybe stuff two or three in my purse.

"I need you to run down to the fruit stand and get some more strawberries from George. Three long cartons should do it. Then swing by the grocery and get some cream cheese. I want to try a recipe I just birthed in my brain with these apples I got left over."

Momma called from the back and I jumped. Her voice wasn't there, then it was. "Yes ma'am," I replied and took the cash envelop from under the register counter. It was meant for purchasing baking needs that momma might need in a rush. I got out a twenty and spread the bill flat and wished that love ran our world. Hoped that it might some day.

"You coming to work the front?" Couldn't abandon my post without knowing momma was coming.

"Yeah! Let me stick these cakes in the oven. You go on. I need them strawberries."

I needed the fresh air away from the chocolate. How was I supposed to control myself? Heading for the door I stalled. A face appeared on the other side. Mr. Expensive had returned to the bakery. This, I hadn't expected. He seemed even more attractive than the image of him I'd saved in my prior memory. Was I distracted by him holding a cupcake? They were also beautiful. Either way he was nice to look at.

"Hello again," I said, feeling butterflies in my stomach as he entered.

"Hello," he replied, his tone polished and deep. I liked that. What girl wouldn't?

"Did you enjoy your cupcake?" I asked.

He grinned. "Yes, did you enjoy yours? I hope you ate them both."

I nodded. "It was delicious. I gave the other to Henry, he's my little brother. Now he asks me for his daily cupcake."

The man's smile was really something else. I wanted him to smile some more. "We have chocolate covered strawberries today. They're a really big hit and oh, we have chocolate raspberry cupcakes. You'd enjoy either or both." I assured him and he seemed convinced.

He tilted his head. "Have you tried those?"

My face flushed and I wanted to lie. But I wasn't a liar so I shook my head. "No, but I smell them and I can promise you this, they are flat yummy and scrumptious."

"Can I help you?" Momma's voice interrupted and I inwardly winced, saying "I gotta go get some strawberries, cream cheese and something else . . ." Quickly I brushed right past him, hurrying through the door. I wasn't about to face momma.

She would take his order and send him on his way. I'd pay for flirting later. She didn't trust men like that. Though Henry's daddy hadn't been anything similar, I really think she's suspicious of men. And I completely understand why.

I headed down the sidewalk towards the grocery to get the cream cheese first. It was the farthest away. I was almost there when I saw Jamie step from the cross-street cleaners to my side. She stopped when she saw me, ducked her had, and hurried down the street. Jamie was obviously avoiding me and we'd never avoided each other. We'd argued before, but never this, Jamie walking in the opposite direction.

I got the cream cheese while worrying about Jamie, wishing I had time to find her, to talk and see what was wrong. It would have to wait until after work because Momma expected me back. I was hoping Mr. Expensive hadn't been asking questions. If he had momma was sure to lecture until I dropped.

George had me several cartons of strawberries already picked and sorted. He must have known it was a strawberry day. We'd sold several dozen already. I figured we'd sell at least eight more before the day was over.

As I paid George I saw Mr. Expensive patiently walking my

way. He held two containers in his hand. It appeared he'd bought my suggestions. Smiling I took the strawberries from George and walked toward this stranger, who was apparently searching for me.

"What did you decide?" I asked him.

He took the grocery bag from my hands and placed a box inside it. He reached for the strawberries, tucked them under his arm and I tell you, that was a load. "I'll help you carry these back."

That was nice but a terrible idea. Momma wasn't going to like that. "You don't have to. I can carry it. I'm sure you have somewhere to be."

He chuckled. "No place as important as helping a lady with her cartons and bag of groceries."

A lady. He called me a lady. I felt very important then. It's silly, but I did.

"I'm used to carrying them. Momma sends me often."

I really needed him to leave. To go on before momma saw us. Even though I wished he could stay. This might be his last time through. Who came to Moulton for a cupcake?

"I'm sure you are. But a man should stop and help. Besides your hands were full and I couldn't very well make you carry one more thing."

Frowning, I glanced up to him. I guessed about six foot three. Much taller than my five foot six. "What else did I need to carry?"

He showed the bag where he had placed his boxes. "Your chocolate strawberries and chocolate raspberry cupcakes. There they are needing consumption."

The man had bought me something again. My mouth watered, even though, I knew I shouldn't take them. Momma would have a fit. Though Henry would love it I bet.

"You bought me something else?" I asked, sounding breathless, highly dramatic and appreciative.

"Yes. Hearing you talk about them with so much passion

made my mouth then water. Figured you should at least get to try them. Shame your mother doesn't allow you a taste test now and then."

"Thank you. Speaking of my momma, she's not going to be happy, that you bought me something again. She thinks I'm flirting and you're buying me treats, because of the flirting I'm doing. Momma has this strange idea about my looks and what they create."

He appeared to be holding back laughter. "And what might they create?"

I sighed and shrugged my shoulders. "She thinks I'm pretty. Over-pretty. But that's not even a word."

When he laughed my face grew hot. I know I turned three shades of red.

Seven

"I 'LL SAVE SOME for Henry. He loved the cupcake," I said the moment Mr. Expensive walked out the door after helping me carry my bundles.

Momma was staring at the box he had left for me on the counter.

"I wasn't even in here momma. I couldn't have flirted with him. He bought those on his own."

She then raised her eyes to meet mine: "he's never worked an honest days labor in his entire trust funded life. His hands are too downy and soft. His skin not damaged by the sun. He wears and smells of easy money. No worry or fear in his eyes. His life has been simple and manageable. He expects to get what he wants because he always has till now. Nothing's ever been a challenge for him. Now, you're something he desires. He's buying you treats that cost him little to draw you in for the kill. That, Sammy Jo, is dangerous. A real man knows work and respect."

Then she turned and went back to the kitchen. Momma was making judgments on a man she didn't know because he'd been kind to me, by giving me gifts and attention. I opened the box to find six strawberries and three gigantic cupcakes. Why three? That, I wondered.

I selected a strawberry and closed my eyes, biting down and allowing the first spray of juice to release inside my mouth. It was as perfect as I'd imagined. And momma's warning was silly I thought. She got upset over nothing. I'd never see the man again. Mr. Expensive was gone.

The door chimed and I spun to see who it was, which was Ben walking inside. I swallowed my bite of strawberry. At least he was here. Maybe he could explain Jamie's behavior that made no sense to me.

"Hey," I said, wiping the juice from my mouth with the back of my hand.

He ducked his head a moment then sighed before looking back at me. "Hey," he responded. "Hey there." As if adding two words made it better.

I knew this was about the lake. It was time we put that behind us. "Are we good?" I asked him, hoping he'd say "yes" and put the thing to rest.

He shrugged. "I don't know. Have you talked to Jamie?"

"Funny you should mention that. I just saw her outside and she all but ran away from me in the street."

His skin paled a shade or two. Something was definitely off.

"Uh . . . yeah . . . well, we kinda . . . just ask her yourself if you want." And he left as quickly as possible.

I picked up a cupcake and watched him hurry off down the street. Things were strange but this cupcake was delicious. A cup of coffee would make it better. No it wouldn't, that's impossible.

"Come get the blueberry bread! Display it right in the front!" Momma called from the back and I replied "yes mam!" tucking my cupcake back into the box and dusting off my hands. I hurried to the kitchen with a smile. I didn't need to remind her about my gifts so I returned to quietly hide them, to make them blend like a regular fixture. Glancing outside I saw Ben pause and look back at the door. Something was strange and though momma would be angry I knew I had to do something about it or it was going to drive me nuts.

"Ben left his change on the counter! I'll be back in a minute!"

"Ben?" she replied. She hadn't seen Ben come in and I didn't have time to explain. He rapidly turned to escape. I ran for the door to yell his name before he climbed in his truck. Ben turned and I hurried right to him. "What's going on?" I asked, sounding breathless and concerned and annoyed. A feat within itself.

He frowned and looked at his boots. There was definitely something wrong. Ben never acted like this.

"Is this about what I said? I'm sorry if I hurt or embarrassed you. I was shocked by what you said. How you assumed things I'd react to. You know me and my mouth, I say what I'm thinking too fast sometimes, but that doesn't affect our friendship."

Ben lifted his head and his eyes met mine. "That's not what's wrong Sammy Jo."

Oh, it isn't, is it? Well, then I was curious as to what it was because Jamie running off was weird. "Would you please tell me because both my friends are treating me strange as of late. I'd like to know why if you please?"

Ben closed his eyes tightly as if the words he would say were going to be painful and hurt me. As if he were safe if I couldn't be seen.

"Jamie's pregnant."

I stood there. He was safe. Eyes still closed, Ben gritting his teeth, the warm summer breeze tangling the hair breaking free of my ponytail, the strands dancing around my face, sticking to the sweat on my brow. I could see Norma Sanders crossing the road with her poodle Josie in the lead. The wafting smell from the bakery crept ever toward me, but even with all that familiarity I was lost, confused and alone. As if I'd stepped into another world. I was Alice down the rabbit hole. Looking skyward from the bottom frozen.

"Wh-what?" I managed to say.

Ben ran his hand over his face and made an odd high-pitched sound. Was he feeling as lost as me? So completely thrown for a loop? When had Jamie even had sex?

"She's pregnant. She told me last night."

She told him, Jamie told Ben, that she was pregnant, but didn't tell me, her best friend on the face of the earth?

"She told you? You?" I repeated, still looking for that clue that this was a dream and couldn't be actually happening.

"Yeah."

"Why? How?" Why had she told him? How was she pregnant? Jamie? Last time I had checked she was a virgin, the two of us in a tiny minority.

I could see the tension in his shoulders. The stress etched on his blood-drained face. His eyes were wide and upward looking. This was as upsetting to him, as it was for me to hear it. Had he asked her these questions? Did he even know the answers? Who was the father of the child?

"We . . . we slept together. Just once. It wasn't planned. We just . . . we . . . it happened. When it was over we swore we'd never tell and things would stay the same. But now, now, it's different. Everything will change because it has to."

My legs felt weak. I wasn't sure I could stand. I was no longer living in reality. "When?" I asked, still not sure, I'd heard him correctly when he said it.

"Last month. The night we were going to Cullman to see a

movie and get something to eat. You had to stay home and keep Henry."

I remembered that night. Henry had fever. Momma had to go into the bakery to do a special order for a wedding. Milly was on a date, such a normal night, nothing strange or life changing at the moment.

But two young lives had been altered. Forever changed, eternally coursed.

"Sammy Jo!" Momma's voice called out. I jerked my head around to see something nearer to a reality where I wasn't uncomfortable. My mother. My angry mother. I had to get back to work.

"I . . . I have to go," I stuttered and instead of trying to figure out the right thing to say at the moment, turned and left him there. "Congratulations" seemed an odd sentiment. Yet they had created a life. One that would blossom in Moulton and know this place as its own. A life that was their responsibility. Something they couldn't take back.

Eight

*T*IME CRAWLED BY the rest of the day and my head was so full of questions and concerns I couldn't even eat the strawberries or cupcakes that Mr. Expensive had left me. My appetite was gone and in its place something that could only be described as fear for my friends had taken over.

I stepped into the evening summer sunshine after work. Momma had agreed I could go visit Jamie. I told her something was wrong and she needed a friend. Momma said to be home by dinnertime. Not much got by her so I figured she knew I was bothered by the interaction she'd interrupted earlier today with Ben. She didn't question me or pause when she agreed.

I took my box of cupcakes and strawberries with me. Maybe Jamie would need a treat. Not that strawberries and cupcakes could fix this. She was eighteen and pregnant with a guy's baby she was just friends with. Dear God, how had I not known they'd been intimate? Had she tried to tell me over the past month and I'd been so wrapped up in my life and dreams that I hadn't been listening? If so, I was a terrible friend. I should have known this.

Been there with her when she took the pregnancy test. She'd done that alone and where was I? Not there. That was where.

I hurried to her house hoping I wouldn't need to track her down. Getting through the past few hours after talking to Ben had been hard. All I'd wanted to do was run to Jamie. Check on her. Talk to her. Make a thing okay that had already happened and would have to be lovingly dealt with.

And also, not to be selfish, but I wanted to stop feeling as if I was going to vomit.

I walked up the front steps of her light blue house that reminded me of a photograph. It wasn't big, but it was cute, the shutters and doors perfectly matching and the woodwork and flowers were immaculate. It was so perfect you knew it wasn't. Something had to be wrong inside. Stopping at the door I stared at the peephole. What was I going to say? Would my words comfort my friend? Was she going to be happy about this? Should I pretend that I didn't know?

I didn't have any answers or suggestions. I reached up and rang the doorbell. Jamie's my best friend, that's always been so. Like family, even closer. She needed me and I was here.

The door opened and there she stood. As if she'd waited behind it. Her face was paler than normal and her eyes seemed larger, sad and sleepless and teary. She was lost inside herself, down in the rabbit hole. Her expression told the truth.

"You talked to Ben?"

I nodded. I wasn't going to lie. I never have and I wouldn't start now.

"And?" she asked.

And? What did she mean by "and?" How did I feel? How was Ben? What? What was she asking? She was scared and hurting. I knew it. I sat the bag holding the box of treats down and then I stepped forward, wrapping my arms around her. That was all I knew to do. She needed comfort. That I could give.

Her stiff body didn't last. Within seconds her shoulders sagged. Jamie embraced me, brought me into her and buried her face in my neck. She twisted her head like a helpless child and we stood like that for a while. Not worried about who saw us.

"He hasn't called since I told him," she said. "Nothing. Not a word."

If I'd known that I might have shook him and yelled when I saw him earlier. Jamie was eighteen and pregnant in Moulton, Alabama. Did he not see how terrified and frightened Jamie was?

"He'll call. He just needs a little space to adjust. And if he doesn't I'll kick his ass." I said it and pulled her tighter.

She sniffled and a laugh escaped. "I should have told you first."

I agreed. But I wasn't going to say that. Not when she was like this. "I have cupcakes and chocolate covered strawberries. Let's go eat them while we talk."

She nodded, then stepped back, her tear filled eyes meeting mine. "I'm scared. Can't quit shaking."

I was also frightened. And it wasn't my life that was about to change. It was hers and Ben's and the child's. "I know," I responded. "I'm here."

I picked up the bag and walked inside a house I knew so well. That smell of apple cinnamon. I always wondered how her mother managed that. Ours always smelled like what momma cooked that day or the day before.

The house was decorated with nice things and always very tidy. Jamie's mom was the expectation of Southern womankind. Married to one man for thirty plus years, come hell or the highest waters. There were decorative pillows on her sofa and fresh flowers on the kitchen table. I liked this house and the way it felt. A knickknack heaven I tell you.

Jamie's dad was the local bank manager and her mother a

stay at home mom. Something momma knew nothing about. She had always worked somewhere. Her income was our keeping. As nice as Jamie's house was I never wanted this life. It wasn't for me, though it fit well for her, so I guess there's balance in everything. I was young and wanted adventure, to get out and see the world. I'd wear fancy clothes and expensive shoes and have my own money to buy them. I'd walk Fifth Avenue in Manhattan, or go shopping in Paris or Rome. Maybe that was selfish and wrong of me, but I had to admit my desires. There's something to be said for my honesty.

We walked up the stairs and opened the first door on the right. Jamie's bedroom was as big as the room I shared with my three sisters. The coral and aqua colored quilt on her bed was what drew your eyes into it, the moment you walked through the door. There were paper balls, the same matching colors, hanging above her bed. Like flowers they gave it a fairytale touch, though our discussion wouldn't be.

All this was safe for Jamie. Safe, until right about now. The room was going to change. Would she put a crib against the wall? Would her parents allow her to live here? Would she marry Ben, make a life of her own and refuse the help of her parents?

"Do you love him?" I gently asked, resting the bag on her dresser.

She sighed and nodded her head. "Yes, I've loved him for years, but he's always just seen you. Until the night that he only saw me." She then pointed at her chest. "The next day it was like it never happened. His eyes were still on you. I kept wishing that wouldn't be the case and he'd continue to just see me."

My chest ached and I wanted to hug her. I hadn't realized until recently that she felt something for Ben. I wish she had told me sooner. Maybe I could've helped by telling Ben how I would never feel that way. But would that end his strange fascination?

Would he ever turn completely to Jamie?

"I was used to boys liking you. They always have. It didn't bother me. You're my best friend and you're beautiful and guys are drawn to that. That's something I always understood. Until Ben. He was my first. The boy I wanted for myself. But it's hard to see me when there's you."

The idea of strawberries and cupcakes no longer appealed to me. I loved Jamie. I didn't want her unhappy. I also wanted to swing at Ben. Break his nose and mash his teeth. Why were guys so dumb? Jamie was sweet, smart, funny and kind, devoted and really pretty. She was an excellent catch. Jamie wanted this life. She'd be a fantastic wife and mother. Didn't Ben see all that? She wanted the same as him. She was perfect for the life he envisioned for himself, but I was the polar opposite. Not only did I not love Ben. I hated Moulton, Alabama.

"I don't think Ben would've slept with you had he not had feelings for you. Right now I imagine he is trying to figure out your future, the two of you. What is best and right for not only you, but the baby growing inside you. He'll call or better yet, come by, if you give him time to think. You know Ben well enough, he'll do the right thing and if he doesn't love you yet, he will fall in love with you soon. I don't doubt that at all. You're easy to love sweetheart."

Jamie sank down onto her bed and sighed as her shoulders sagged. "What if he hates me forever?"

That idea was ludicrous. "Hate you? Because he chose to have sex with you, without using protection? That wasn't your fault, excuse me, but there were two people present that night."

Jamie lifted her head and her eyes were so sad it broke my heart to see it: "I told him I was on the pill. I have been for my irregular periods. But I knew they weren't strong. My doctor explained that it was enough to keep my periods regular, but not a great form of protection. I knew that, and . . . and . . . I didn't take my pill that night. I can tell myself a million times it was an accident and I forgot. But deep down, I don't think that it was. I think I meant for this to happen."

If she had meant for this to happen it had been a fleeting fantasy. Now she was faced with reality. I didn't think Jamie premeditated trapping Ben as a father. However, if she had, then Jamie's future may be exactly what she wanted.

"Doesn't matter now. You're going to have a baby. And you're going to be an excellent mother. That kid is a lucky egg."

A small smile touched her lips and I hoped I was right. For all three of the people included.

Nine

I HADN'T PLANNED on going to the barn dance but after a week of leaving work to check on Jamie and lift her spirits I figured she needed me there. Ben hadn't asked her to go, although he had finally called her and they had met late one evening to talk about things in his truck. He hadn't made any promises yet, but he had mentioned marriage.

Jamie needed to pretend as if life were normal. Being the good friend that I was I had momma alter my nicest dress that she made for last year's dance. My breasts were bigger and my hips flared more. I couldn't tell, but it had happened. She also added a satin belt that tied in a pretty bow. I was asked by four different boys to go and I'd turned them all down in a row. If it weren't for Jamie, I wouldn't be going. I didn't really want to dance with any boys from Moulton, Alabama.

Momma was pleased I was going. She didn't understand why Jamie was my date, but she seemed positive about the fact I'd be there with local boys, preening and showing themselves. I picked up the blueberry cobbler she had just finished baking and put it on the cake plate that set in the center of the display. I would smell it for the next eight hours. Good thing blueberry cobbler wasn't one of my favorites. I'd also had momma's several times at home. It wouldn't be torture, just agony.

The doorbell chimed, the door then opened, and Mr. Expensive was there. I had questions: why are you here? Do you work nearby? What is your name? But I didn't ask a one. That would be flirting and momma would hear me. I glanced back to make sure the kitchen door was closed. I wanted momma to stay back there, instead of coming out here and being rude.

"Good morning," I said with a smile, reassuring myself that the door was shut and that momma was safely busy.

"Good morning," he replied with a grin. He had impressive straight white teeth. I'd never seen teeth so perfect.

"You must be working nearby. We don't normally get out of towners repeating their business this soon." I said it without asking a question.

He smirked. "Actually no, I don't. But after my first visit I keep getting drawn back here. Regularly."

I wanted to think that comment was meant for me. But I'd had my momma's baking and knew it was meant for the treats. "My momma can have that affect."

He stopped on the other side of the counter and studied me for a moment. I wanted to fidget and fix my hair. Make sure my breath was clean and that nothing was out of place. He seemed so polished and perfect. Was he finding all my flaws?

"I'm sure your mother brings in tons of people with her talented baking. However, I was referring to you."

I wanted to respond, but what do I say, flirting wasn't my habit, something I practiced daily. Now I wished I had practiced more. It could be helpful at a time like this.

"I've made you nervous. Surely you get attention from the

men in this town on a regular basis?"

Men, no, not men, I wouldn't call the boys here men. They were still drinking beer and swimming in the lake and none of them had a goal to be more than Moulton offered.

"Honestly, other than work here and at home, I don't go out much."

Now I sounded completely boring.

"Your mother's smart. If she let you out you'd be married within the year."

I laughed. My momma would love for me to be married. I shook my head. "No, that's not it. I just don't want this life. I plan to get out of Moulton, out of Alabama for good. I want to see the world. Not marry a farmer and have a bunch of babies just like everyone else."

He smiled and bit his lip. Not one I'd seen before. People around here always mocked me, grinning with spite and arrogance. As if I was dreaming too big. His smile was more appreciative.

"What's your number one?" he asked.

"My what?"

"The first place on your list of places you want to see."

Oh, well, that was hard. But I would have to say "New York. Manhattan to be exact."

"Fifth Avenue?" he added, reading my mind.

I nodded.

"It's a nice place to visit but not to live. I tried it once and only lasted a year before I headed back to Tennessee."

Tennessee? He lived in Tennessee? That was a let down. Although I was sure he lived in a nice big house somewhere expensive. It was still the south. He looked like he belonged somewhere bigger. Brighter. Shinier.

"You look disappointed," he said. He was either very perceptive or I was just easy to read.

"Oh, no. I just didn't expect you to live in Tennessee. I was surprised."

He let out a chuckle then turned his attention to the display. "What do you suggest today?"

He was changing the subject and I was so thankful I moved over to the case and opened it up. "The chocolate cupcakes have raspberry cream inside. Fresh raspberries are in them also. The cobbler is nice and warm." I couldn't even sell the cobbler to him. I was terrible. He might not even buy me something today. I should have tried harder with the cobbler. It was delicious. It just wasn't a mystery.

"I'll take four cupcakes," he replied.

I boxed them and placed them on the counter. "Coffee?" I asked him.

"Please."

After fixing his coffee I handed it to him. "Nine dollars and fifteen cents," I told him.

He reached into his wallet and pulled out a twenty, guiding it across the counter. "I don't need the change," he said. He then opened his box and lifted a cupcake, which left me three again. I wanted to ask him why three, but he turned to exit the bakery. I watched him retreat, then stop, revolving to look right at me. It made my stomach do a little flip.

"Thank you for the cupcakes," I said, quickly before I forgot.

"I have a penthouse in Manhattan, Chicago and Boston. A cabin in Colorado, and a townhouse in San Francisco." Then he tuned and left. Just like that. As if nothing more needed to be added, said or otherwise mentioned. I myself had nothing to add. I lived in a room with my sisters. Sometimes we confused our panties. I couldn't imagine having five residences. Or even having a room to myself.

Ten

S TRINGS OF WHITE lights covered the ceiling of the large barn in Moulton's center. It was here before the town and as a historical monument was well preserved and tended. Town events happened here. The doors were slid open in the back and front inviting the warm evening breeze. The trees outside were also decorated, the live music that was playing from the make shift stage was just inside the barn.

Colorful flowers were placed like a maze around the stage and through both entries. These led you to dance and to the drinks and snacks, but they were sure to trip a few. Girls were in their dresses and boots or heels while the guys were all in jeans, their plaid shirts as stiff as boards. Laughter mixed with the music from Herman Borris's band and it all seemed very typical. The usual. Nothing new.

Jamie looked toward the drink table. "Do you think the punch has already been spiked? I smell cornmash in the air like incense. It's a moonshine evening for sure."

Probably. "You had better stick with water or sweet tea," I responded.

She nodded in agreement. I had hoped all day that Ben would call her and ask Jamie to the dance tonight. I kept scanning the crowd for a sign of him or his truck around the square. I was trying to let him adjust and make a plan, but right now I wanted to wring his neck for his immature behavior and neglecting my best friend. Jamie was dressed in a lovely white chiffon dress that stopped at her knees and was strapless. It came straight off the rack of a department store in Cullman. She paid over one hundred dollars for it and she looked gorgeous.

Ben shouldn't be missing this.

I watched as she looked through the crowd. She was nervous and the way she kept fidgeting with her dress made me want to pop her hand. She didn't need to be nervous. She needed to walk around like the beauty she was and own that. Be as natural as possible under the circumstances and enjoy an evening with me.

"Do you think he'll come?" she asked. I reached down to take the hand that was picking the ruffled chiffon. I squeezed until she squeezed back.

"If he doesn't then he's missing out. You look amazing. Dance with everyone who asks and enjoy yourself."

She nodded without looking convinced.

I saw Cole Marsh walking our way and his eyes were on me. Crap.

"Hello ladies," he said, not acknowledging Jamie's existence, except for making ladies plural. That infuriated me so I attacked.

"Cole," I said in a voice that didn't sound pleased or inviting. "You ass," I quietly mumbled, Cole not hearing a thing.

"You look gorgeous as always," he said. I turned my gaze away and winced.

"Thanks," I muttered. "Imbecile." I was disgusted with men in general.

"Herman's got it rolling up there. Want to join me for a go on the dance floor?"

"No thanks." I then cut my eyes back at him. I actually felt them flash. If he asked Jamie now I'd be pissed. That was an obvious diss. Like the dumbass he obviously was, he finally looked at Jamie. "What about you? Want to dance?"

She glanced at me and knew me well enough that the frown on my face meant that saying "yes" was a bad idea.

"No thanks. We just got here and I'd like to go get a drink first."

The smart thing for Cole to do at that moment was to offer to go get her a drink. Then maybe she would dance with him. But instead he sighed and shook his head. "Alright, shoot a man down why don't ya." Then he walked off like a child.

"He's a jerk," I said. "An asshole."

"I agree," she replied.

"Let's go get you something to drink. Wait for a better option."

She nodded and we headed for the drink table. I decided I wanted some punch, because if I was going to get through tonight without slugging someone's face, I would require some home brew to do it. To settle me down a bit. Momma would have a fit if she found out, but one drink wouldn't hurt. Besides, the punch isn't supposed to be spiked. It just always is, so I drink it.

"He's here," Jamie whispered, almost panicked, her hand gripping my arm. I followed her gaze and found Ben walking, dressed in jeans and a new plaid shirt, like the rest of the guys in the barn. Why the hell do they wear the same thing? He glanced at me a moment before his eyes went to Jamie. I knew she looked beautiful, though she didn't realize it, which is both good and bad together.

I could see the appreciation in his eyes. I figured he might dance with her. That and the fact she was having his baby. Sweet mother! I needed a drink!

"What do I do?" she asked nervously.

"You go get a drink like you planned." I told her bluntly and led her to the drinks. "Don't look at him. Make him come to you."

I wasn't sure of the origin of my matchmaking tips but they were there like I knew what I was doing. We made it to the drink table before Ben got to us and then he closed rather quickly.

"Hello," he said cautiously, like he was afraid of something. Perhaps me, which was a good idea. I then nudged Jamie to respond.

"Hi," she said with a shaky breath.

"You look beautiful," and I knew his words were real, not forced or just pretended. He gained a few points there. Not enough yet, but a few. He had a lot of humbling to do.

"Thanks," she said softly. I knew Jamie well enough to know she wasn't sure she believed him at that moment. I wished she'd see herself the way others saw her beauty.

"Getting something to drink? Or would you like to dance?" He asked her and it was sincere.

Again, I barely moved my arm, but the pinch I gave her side was enough of a nudge to enliven her. She understood what I was saying.

"Uh, yeah, I'd like to dance," she replied.

Ben looked at me and nodded a greeting. "I'm going to steal her away," he told me. "We'll find you directly pal."

"Good," was my response.

That made him smile and released me. Maybe things would be okay.

I fixed myself a glass of punch. Sure enough the nip of the

homebrew set my throat to tingling. That was good. A positive thing. At least I could make it through the night. It would loosen me up enough to dance with a guy or two. Ben was showing Jamie he wasn't going anywhere. He needed to do more than ask her to dance, but that was a start I guess.

"I understand that events like this don't offer alcohol. Not legally anyway." A deep voice spoke close to my ear and I jumped because I was startled. Luckily, my punch didn't spill on my dress, nor did I spin and swing.

Turning, I came face to face with Mr. Expensive grinning, the man biting his lower lip, as pleased to be in my presence, for I was aglow in his.

Eleven

E WASN'T DRESSED in jeans and a plaid shirt. Not even close. Instead, his pants were a dark gray and probably cost more than my mother's monthly salary. The white, long sleeved button down shirt he was wearing was casual, the sleeves rolled to his elbows with his top button undone. Like he was just getting comfortable after a long day of work.

Not only did he look expensive, he smelled expensive also.

And all of that, added to the fact that he lived a life I dreamed about made me a little giddy. I hadn't expected to see him. How he had known about this dance was beyond me. But I didn't care. All I cared about was that he was here.

"The punch," I told him. "The alcohol is in the punch."

"Ahh, so they hide the good stuff," he replied.

I handed him my cup. "It's moonshine, rotgut, like diesel fuel. Go gently dear friend. Be cautious."

He chuckled, took my drink and drank deeply like the booze was well water. Not even a wince. I guess just because he was wealthy didn't take away from his Tennesseeness.

"I'll get another," I told him. "You can have that one."

"Is this a secret everyone knows or do some find out the hard way?" he asked.

"They all know. They just pretend they don't. God fearing Baptists and all."

He took another drink and I went to pour myself a cup. The clear plastic containers didn't hold nearly enough. When I returned, yes, he was present.

"You're here?" I stated the obvious, but it felt like a question and so was stated as such.

He grinned. "It would appear that way."

I put the cup to my lips and took a long sip. I tried to hide my smile but it was difficult. He made me feel happy. Like there was hope or excitement in my future. Like I was new, not waiting on a shelf.

"I noticed the fliers all over town when I was in the other day to get a cupcake. Figured I might get lucky and you'd be here. And your mother, she, would not."

This time I laughed. I didn't even try to hide my amusement. "My momma can be a tricky one to escape."

He looked thoughtful a moment then turned his head toward me. "I'm trying to figure out how you're not already out there on some guys arm."

This time I smirked. "I don't want to be."

"Any reason why?"

"They're all staying here. No one leaves. They all stay. I don't want that."

"And what do you want?" he asked.

I thought that was obvious. I wanted out of this place. But instead I said the following: "I want to know your name."

He chuckled and extended his hand. "Hale Christopher Jude III," he replied. "Will you do me the honor of a dance Sammy

Jo Knox?"

He surprised me by knowing my full name. I didn't have time to play his over in my head like I wanted to. It sounded wealthy. Like he was important.

I slipped my hand into his and his fingers wrapped around mine with gentle strength. I liked that. It made me feel as if I was his and I realized being Hale Christopher Jude III's didn't sound bad at all. It sounded more like a fairytale. You don't see the night in the light. That's a thing I will have to remember.

He led me to the dance floor where his hands found my waist and rested there as if he were staking his claim. I put mine on his shoulders and tilted my head, just enough to meet his eyes. He had beautiful eyes. Ones that absorbed and drew you inside them and once you were there all else seemed still and that was fine with me.

"When do you turn nineteen?" He asked as he began to move us with the music, our bodies swaying just so that they brushed the other, like eyelashes sweeping a cheek.

He knew my age. He knew my name. How? How did he know that? The man had barely come into town three times and only then to stop at the bakery. No one here seemed to know him. I did a quick glance around to see if anyone was watching us and realized that most everyone was. It wasn't because they knew him. It was the exact opposite. He was a stranger. A rich stranger that currently had me in his arms, everyone knowing I wanted out of Moulton, the crowd waiting to see if I ran off tonight and never came back to this place. The silliness of such a thought. I wanted out, but I wasn't escaping, with a man I didn't even know.

"How do you know my name and age?"

His lips turned up at the edges. He gave me an innocent shrug. It didn't seem to fit the worldly man dancing to my front. "After the first time I saw you in the bakery I made an inquiry.

Does that bother you?"

No, not exactly. But I wanted to know who was asked. I thought about probing for more, but I didn't for some odd reason.

"August tenth," I told him.

He looked thoughtful. "Do you have plans for college?"

I wanted to laugh at that question. My mother worked at a bakery. How did he expect me to afford college? I didn't even own a car.

"No, I'll work at the bakery until . . ." and I didn't finish the sentence.

"Until?" He wasn't going to allow me to leave that hanging.

"Until I can escape here."

The music changed and the song slowed. He slid a hand around to the small of my back and eased me closer to him. His body was tight against mine. I wanted to stay like this.

"How were you planning to escape?" His voice had dropped to a low husky whisper and I shivered at the sound, a creep up my back that was pleasant and lasting, well past the words he'd spoken.

"I don't know," I told him. Telling him the truth would sound bad. Letting him know that the only real plan I had at the moment was getting a man to take me from here sounded desperate. He may think I was going to sink my claws into him and use him for my escape route. The truth was, I would leave on my own if I could.

"I think you do," he replied.

I looked over his shoulder to hide my expression. I wasn't good at concealing my thoughts. My gaze landed on Jamie and Ben, now huddled closely together, talking away from the dance floor. Ben's hand was on her left cheek, Jamie clinging to his every word. Things were going to be okay for them. Maybe this wasn't how Jamie wanted to start her life, but she loved Ben and that was enough. For some it wasn't enough. For me love wasn't enough. But for those two it would be, because they shared the same dream, the same wants. The same expectations and fears.

"I'm not calling you a liar," he said, gently bending close to my ear. "I can see the intelligence in your eyes. You've thought about this for years. Possibly since you were old enough to know you wanted more. So I know you have a plan."

Something about him made me want to tell him everything. Even if it may send him running from me and Moulton. It wasn't like I intended to trap him. I didn't want to leave with just any man that came along. I glanced back at Ben and Jamie. I wanted that too. The intimacy of having someone near. Of knowing you were wanted and loved.

"It's not a plan exactly. It's a dream. A hope I want to reveal." I then turned my eyes back to his. "I want to fall in love. Not with a boy here, but with someone who wants to travel the world. Someone with more ambition than to build a house with a white picket fence and have babies till their uterus falls out."

That was the truth and he laughed, saying nothing in response to the statement. The song ended and a fast one began. He slipped his hand into mine and we walked off the floor. I was aware of the eyes on our faces. I felt self-conscious, but that shouldn't be, we weren't stealing away to go vanish.

We both had a glass of punch and my tension eased a smidge. He asked about my job at the bakery, my sisters, and my mom. The punch made me chatty. Or it was my nerves. I wasn't sure which one. I should've probably downed another.

After I had answered all his questions he stood up and thanked me for the dance. Then he left. Nothing more. No promises of seeing him again. No kiss. No embrace. No wink. Hale Christopher Jude III simply walked away.

Twelve

*I*T WAS ALL over town within a week. Everyone had seen it and if they hadn't seen it they had witnessed the glow of pure joy on Jamie's face when she passed. The tiny diamond wasn't enough to sparkle, but her smile was fifty of them.

Ben and Jamie were engaged. He had asked her on her front door step two nights ago on his knee. She said yes and promptly got in her car and hurried to my house to show me the ring he had slid on her finger. The fear from last week was gone and in its place was hope and excitement, for a future yet unlived.

"I know this doesn't sound appealing to you, but Sam, it's all I've ever wanted. I'm getting to live my own fairytale," she had said, tears welling in her eyes.

I hugged her tightly and told her she deserved this fairytale. I couldn't think of a princess more deserving of her prince and then she bawled. I did not dread for her future, because she'd never wanted anything apart from this town and what it offered to her parents. I understood that and it was okay, my dreams being different, because we're all unique, two people being rarely alike.

Now they were looking at houses for rent. He had gotten a second job working with his father and Jamie had gotten one too. That was the only way they could pay their own bills and she seemed happy going everyday. I wished she could work with me at the bakery, but they had all the employees they needed.

Gossip about the stranger in town had spread, but thankfully that ended with the news of the engagement, which halted everyone's predictions about me running off with the man. Momma had gotten wind of it and drilled me with questions about him. All I had was his name, his residences and his smell. Maybe it was the punch, but he had asked me all kinds of things and not once had I thought to ask him something about himself. That could have been why he left like he did. He realized I was self-absorbed and he wanted more than that in a woman. I wouldn't blame him if that were the case. Normally, I was more inquisitive, but with him I had been so focused on answering him properly I hadn't thought about the fact the conversation was all about me. And let's face it. I was boring. Hale probably had to stop and get coffee to wake him up and get him home after all my talking. Sighing, I picked up the bucket of corn that I had just shucked and headed for the house. Momma had the other girls inside making fried pies that she sold at the church auction last Sunday. People would start picking up their fresh pies this afternoon.

It was a fundraiser for the church. I figured momma should sell the fried pies herself and make her own money, but she frowned when I mentioned it, like I had just said a curse word. Henry was inside on a chair watching the others closely as they worked at the kitchen table and the counter tops.

"Get that corn put away, then help clean up in here. There's flour all over the place. We don't need it looking this messy when folks come to pick up their pies. I need you to take Mrs. Winters and Harriet and old man Garth their pies. They do good to make it to the church house on Sunday, God bless their shut in souls."

I grabbed the broom and started sweeping after putting the corn in the pantry. The church auction happened about three to four times a year depending on how much money they needed if the tithing were insufficient. Folks may have a hard time putting their money in an offering plate the way the Bible tells them to, but they sure didn't have a hard time buying momma's friend pies with it. Or the other baked goods that were auctioned off. They liked getting something for their money other than a promise of blessings. That, they could not eat. For this momma would slap my face.

Momma always said this wouldn't be needed if they'd all just read their Bibles and follow the rules as written. I figured if the Bible was full of rules then no wonder they didn't want to read it. I liked the stories in it, especially the romantic ones, though often weirdly violent. I wasn't much of a fan of the rules though.

"Give me a bite pwease?" Henry begged as he watched them spoon the blueberry and sugar mixture into the kneaded dough.

"Don't you start that Henry. Those aren't for us. Go get a rag and help Sammy Jo clean the counter tops."

I didn't understand why it was such a big deal. Henry should get at least one little pie. He didn't understand all this giving to the Lord stuff. He was a baby. If momma didn't have them so damndably accounted, I would sneak him a big pie later. But she'd know it was missing and I'd end up confessing and have to listen to he rant.

"You seen that rich man again since the barn dance?" Bessy asked, flashing a mischievous smile over her lowered shoulder. She knew bringing that up in front of momma would only cause me grief.

"I wish I could have seen him," Hazel added wistfully.

Milly loosed a sigh then rolled her eyes. "He wasn't a big deal.

People talk too much. I doubt he was even wealthy. Just because he was dressed up don't make him rich." The annoyance in her voice was hard to miss.

"You're just jealous he didn't dance with you," Bessy said.

"So he could run off and leave me alone at the dance for the whole town to see? No thank you. I was happy with my date who took me home and walked me to my door."

This wasn't a competition. But to Milly most things were. I ignored it and finished my chores.

"Everyone knows Sammy Jo is the prettiest girl in town. He'll be back," Bessy declared.

I didn't look to see Milly's reaction. She hated it when our appearances were mentioned. I thought Milly was pretty. I wasn't anything special. We had a lot of the same features. But no one had ever acted as if they needed to protect Milly from the world of men. Me, on the other hand, momma had been different with. Like I required special protection.

"That's enough," Momma said, stopping the conversation before it got worse. "We've got pies to make and work to do. No talking about boys and dating. That's nonsense unless you got a ring on your finger."

"Like Jamie does," Hazel chimed in with excitement.

Momma nodded. "Yes, like Jamie."

Thirteen

*J*AMIE WAS MAKING wedding plans and Ben had stopped glaring at me in the way that made me nervous. He was marrying Jamie and respected that. I even saw affection in his gaze when he looked at her. It made things easier and more difficult for us all at the same time. I had suddenly become the third wheel or at least I felt that way. Our easy friendship was no longer. Jamie was my best friend and Ben was now her fiancé.

My world here was changing and it was time. It was time it changed for all of us. The idea of my best friends having a baby was exciting. Seeing them go from the kids we were to parents was something they both wanted and they were happy about it. Personally, myself, I was ready for something different, for my own selfish plans to unfold. Seeing them start their life anew made me want to do the same. That just meant getting out of here. Which was a lot more difficult without the means and the means meant more money.

This morning I had to walk to the bakery. Momma left early so I chose to walk, the exercise was good for me, and being out of doors, instead of in the bakery, would help with having to sit inside staring at the walls all day.

Soon friends would start going off to college. Even if it wasn't a college far away, it was still somewhere else. I wanted to do the same, that being the best of my options. But I wasn't scholarship material and momma couldn't afford tuition or board or even qualify for the basic loans. She also needed my help at the bakery and I just couldn't leave her twisting.

A car slowed down beside me. I turned my head to see a black Mercedes, a sedan all slick and gleaming. The passenger's window lowered automatically and there was Hale Christopher Jude III as present as the clouds in the sky.

"Good morning," he said, with that smile that was almost too perfect.

"Morning," I replied, smiling also. Apparently he hadn't been bored enough to stay away too long. "You in town for a cupcake?" I asked him.

He gave me a small shrug. "That wouldn't be a bad idea, but I was actually hoping to talk to you."

Oh. "Okay," I said, slowing to a stop as he did.

"Want to get in?"

I was taught not to get into a car with strangers. But this wasn't a stranger. Sure, I knew very little about him, but I did know enough I guess. Or at least I thought I did. Opening the door I climbed inside wondering if anyone was watching. The idea of my mother standing outside the bakery ready to scold me in front of Hale made me anxious. But this was definitely worth it. The smell that met me was his cologne and the luxurious smell of new car. I inhaled twice rather deeply.

"Did you enjoy the rest of the evening at the dance?"

I didn't stay after he left, but I wasn't sure I should tell him that. It made me sound pathetic. "The punch made everything enjoyable," I joked and he chuckled in response: "yeah, I guess that would help. However, the little I was there, I enjoyed it completely sober."

I felt my cheeks warm and blush. "It sure was a surprise you being there," I said, expertly ducking my head so my cheeks weren't on display.

"Really? I would have thought my interest was obvious. Do you think I actually come into town so often for cupcakes? Surely you've realized my visits are about you."

This was my Cinderella moment. I wanted to take a photo, or better yet video this. Have it as a memory so when it was over I could remember it actually happened. I needed to respond appropriately. He was polished and refined and worldly. I didn't need to remind him I wasn't by saying stupid things. I liked him coming around and I'd deal with momma in time.

"Honestly, I thought you came through here on your way to work and liked the coffee and cupcakes."

He laughed. I hoped that was a good laugh. One that meant he was really amused and not making me feel better about my true, but goofy response.

"That's what I like about you. You're so innocent and sweet. Women who are generally as beautiful as you are never either of those. At least not in my experience."

I wasn't beautiful like the women in his world. They had money to make them even more beautiful. But as he measured me next to them it made me smile, feel special and adore him.

"Can I take you to dinner? I enjoyed the dance immensely. But I'd like to spend some time with you, so we can talk and get to know each other, without the loud music and sets of eyes staring directly at us."

Momma wasn't going to like this. I would handle that. If I had to lie about where I was going I would do that in a second.

This was a great opportunity. I didn't want to miss this. Hale could be my future.

"I would love to," I told him, trying not to smile too brightly, appearing psychotic and then scaring him away, leaving me, again, in Moulton.

"Tonight? Seven?"

I wasn't sure how to pull this off. "Yes. Seven sounds good." I would have all day to scheme, to figure out how to handle momma.

He pulled up to the bakery and parked the car. "I'll pick you up here? Or at home?"

Good question. If I had to lie to momma, then him coming to my house was potentially disastrous. But if he picked me up here someone could see us and tell her within a minute.

Letting him sit to wait on my response wasn't helping matters in the least. I needed to make a decision. "My house," I blurted, reaching into my purse, bringing out a receipt and pen. I had to give him directions. He had a fancy GPS, but my home was on a dirt road and I was sure it wouldn't assist him. "Here, I wrote my address on the side, but I seriously doubt a GPS can track poverty into a holler. Sorry, I meant a hollow."

He nodded, chuckled and tucked it in his pocket. "I'll see you at seven crazy."

"Okay." Before I opened the door and got out I knew momma would have to be faced, sooner, rather than later, if she saw me leaving this car. "And you'll probably have to come inside and talk to momma," I told him, apologetically hanging my head.

He grinned: "never doubted that. Knew that was coming from the start."

Fourteen

I WAS FORTUNATE enough that momma didn't see me exiting Hale's car. This gave me all morning to work and prepare my case for when I asked her about tonight. She wanted us to be married and have the lives we wanted. I just needed her to realize Hale could very well become that. Then again, he may just be another guy with interest, but he could also be more I thought. I needed the chance to find out.

When the door chimed from the last morning customer I knew I had a gap, the after lunch crowd still a ways off and I intended to deal with momma. I needed to talk to her before my sisters heard it. Their opinions on the subject weren't required, though they would require their airing, to any and all that would listen. They were nosy let me tell you.

I straightened my apron, adjusted my hair and made sure my hands were clean. I was preparing to approach my mother and didn't want my appearance distracting. She liked me to look a certain way for the customers and for myself. Sometimes I forgot to straighten my apron or wash flour from my hands. That annoyed the woman. Before I went back I took a peek at the mirror set into the wall behind me. Deciding I was good I headed to the kitchen where I could smell the banana nut bread baking as she worked on an order. That was a treat she'd make for us every once and awhile. Especially if the bananas over ripened. Momma didn't believe in throwing away food. She'd find a use every time.

The door swung open then closed. Momma turned her head and glanced at me over her floured shoulder. "Sprinkle those doughnuts with powdered sugar. Go turn on the doughnuts sign."

Great. Not good timing. "I was going to ask you something."

"Doughnuts don't stay hot forever. Get them sold," she replied.

I didn't want to anger her so I did as I was told and went back out to the front. I put them on display, turned on the sign, and sure enough within ten minutes five customers came right in. We were down to a dozen when Mayor Harley bought them "for the office." From the looks of the man I imagined he was hiding in his car with a glass of milk shoving them down his throat. Doughnuts weren't something momma did often. They brought in people fast, selling out within the hour. The specialty sign we'd put in the glass made the doughnuts vanish quickly. "Okay, let's try this again." I turned off the sign after Mr. Harley left and once again prepared myself.

She was stirring her large mixing bowl, but there was nothing coming out of the oven. Again, she glanced at me. "Special order?" she asked.

"No ma'am. It's quiet after the doughnuts. Mr. Harley just bought the last dozen."

Momma made a tsk-tsk sound. Shook her head and frowned. "Hope he doesn't eat them all. The man's gonna keel over and die if he keeps on eating like he does."

"Yeah," I agreed.

"What is it you're needing of me?" Momma wasn't one to waste time. She didn't believe in procrastination and idling was when the devil worked.

"The wealthy man that comes in here . . ."

"The one that showed up at the dance? Has he been back today?"

I nodded. "Yes ma'am, he has, and I really like him. He's successful and . . ."

" . . . he's rich and saw your face and just can't stay away. Thinks he can buy anything he wants and that now includes you."

This was not going well. "No, it's not like that. He's generous and thoughtful and he makes me laugh and he asks questions about me. He rarely talks about himself."

Momma continued to stir, while her frown did not lift. "He's asked you out on a date?"

I nodded. "Yes. And I want to go. It's tonight at seven and I gave him directions to our house so you can meet him. He likes me momma and he's . . . not from here in Moulton."

She sighed and sat the bowl down. "Him not being from Moulton is what's most important to you. You can't pick a man because of his address. Love happens or it don't. Men with that kind of money love their way of life, love buying what they want, not necessarily what they need. That having been said I knew one day you'd catch the eye of a rich man. If I say no you'll go anyway, even walk right out the door. So let him come. I'll talk to the man. Just remember Sammy Jo, not all fairy tales are real, true or wise. Firstly, they are tales. There's more to a man than his money and what he can gift you with his wallet. It's his heart that matters most."

Momma rarely said this many words. She wasn't one to waste time. Even if I didn't agree, I listened because she was my mother. She'd been hurt by a man and it showed. Sure he had left her Henry, and the boy was worth it all, but momma didn't trust men. Not since daddy died. She felt betrayed in his death and the absence of another and that can't leave you any strength, except to trudge through the day.

"Yes ma'am. Thank you," I replied. I really wanted to do a little dance, but that could wait until I was alone to save the humiliation.

"Go on now before Deloris shows up. She'll want the rest of the raspberry tarts for her dessert tonight."

I didn't argue. I was shocked that this had been easy. If momma didn't have the highest hopes for my future with Hale in the long run, at least I would have the experience. Dating wasn't something I did much of because I didn't have a pool to choose from. They were all here for life. This was my first chance at something outside of Moulton, Alabama. Even if the night was a failure at least I had that chance.

When I got back to the front Deloris was walking inside. It was just like momma had predicted. I boxed up her raspberry tarts with a silly grin on my face. I couldn't help it, I was silly and excited, my life shifting towards the positive.

The next five customers kept me busy and moving. They were buying their after dinner treats and asking questions about momma's baking, what we would have tomorrow. Almost two hours passed before I got a chance to sit on my stool and think. What will I wear? How to fix my hair? Where would we go on the date? All of that had my head spinning, until four rolled around and we closed the doors and headed home for the evening. Momma didn't say one word about Hale on our drive or when we arrived. She was quiet. Uncomfortably so.

Fifteen

OR A GIRL with a very limited wardrobe I managed to change clothes five times. Keeping tonight a secret from my sisters was impossible. Especially since I borrowed Milly's black skirt. Milly wasn't there and when she got home I was going to be in trouble, but I was willing to face the wrath of my sister to look nice tonight.

Bessy was the first to notice my skirt when I walked into the kitchen.

"Pretty," Henry said, beaming up at me. At least I was appreciated by the only male in the family.

"Milly's gonna kill you," Bessy sang in a sing song voice.

"I'll make it up to her. My clothes are free for her to borrow anytime she wants."

Momma was organizing the pantry with all the canning we had done. She paused and turned to look at me. I was prepared for her to tell me to take Milly's skirt off and if that was the case I had a back up. It wasn't as perfect as this, but it would do.

"I reckon I bought that skirt for Milly's graduation. She can share. Lord knows she's asked to borrow enough since she started dating."

I exhaled a sigh of relief. I wasn't going to have to change. If momma said I could wear it, then I knew I was going to be safe.

Bessy clicked her tongue. "She still ain't gonna be happy."

Momma waved her hand as if that didn't matter and went back to the pantry.

"When is he getting here?" Bessy asked. She was almost as anxious as me. She hadn't seen Hale before and only knew him as the cupcake guy. I wasn't sure I trusted her and what she might say, although I didn't have a choice. It wasn't like momma would let me lock her in a closet.

"Seven," I told her.

"Momma said his name is Hale. Not cupcake man," she said grinning.

"Cupcakes?" Henry's eyes lit up at the word and he looked at me hopefully.

"No cupcakes tonight buddy," I told him, ruffling his blonde curls.

Henry's smile collapsed and I wished I had something to give him.

"No need for cupcakes tonight. I'm making banana nut bread. The bananas are getting too ripe. I need to stop buying them if y'all aren't going to eat them. The grapes get gone though. Figures y'all would eat the expensive fruit." Momma spoke from the pantry like she was speaking to herself and not a one of us were listening.

"You aren't wearing much makeup," Bessy said, changing the subject and bringing things back to my date. Not exactly what I wanted.

"She don't need makeup," momma replied.

Bessy sighed and crossed her arms over her chest. "It's not

fair that Sammy Jo got all the looks. She barely left any for the rest of us. I need makeup."

Bessy had been going on about wearing makeup for a year. She argued that the other girls in her grade were wearing it. Momma didn't care about other girls, or what people thought in general. Bessy should know better than that. But silliness was Bessy's biggest flaw. I hoped she grew out grew it.

Hazel walked in from the back yard, the screen door closing behind her. She was carrying a basket of corn. When she saw me she stopped and smiled. "Wow, you look beautiful."

"See," Bessy said, pointing at me. "She got all the looks. Don't be too mesmerized, or expect the rest of us to stun you, because none of us look like her."

Momma sighed in exasperation and gave Bessy a warning: "that's enough from you and that mouth."

I glanced at the clock above the table and it was exactly seven. My nerves were already frayed. But this made it worse, because he was near, and would be here any minute. What if I wasn't dressed nice enough? These were the nicest clothes I could assemble.

"Oh my lord! Would you look at that car!" Bessy blurted and ran to the window. She peered outside at the vehicle that we could all hear approaching the house. I was relieved he had found my home and equally ready to vomit from the wad that rested in my stomach. Before Bessy opened her mouth I wanted to get him away. That was my main goal.

"That's enough. Heat the oven and grab the biscuits. They're on the iron skillet in the freezer. Put those vegetables into the crock pot," Momma told Bessy rudely. She was making her busy to soothe me.

"Go on and get the front door and I'll be there in a minute to meet the man."

I wanted to go hug momma and thank her for being

completely awesome. She knew Bessy was going to act ridiculous so she kept her occupied.

"Thank you," I murmured, hurrying past them into the living room where the front door was. We never used that door. We always came through the back, directly into the kitchen.

I watched from the window as Hale walked the sidewalk and managed the worn wooden steps of my porch. Although momma stained and sealed them once a year they were still aging. Daddy built that porch when I was just a kid. The shade the old oak provided kept the sun from wearing it completely. Otherwise it would have fallen apart.

I expected him to be in slacks or something fancy. The jeans and cotton polo he was wearing came as a surprise. A good one. That meant I wasn't under dressed. I figured his jeans probably cost a fortune, but they were still jeans. The pink and yellow roses in his hand made my cheeks flush. I'd never been given flowers like that. Sure, I'd had a rose or a daisy given to me at school on Valentine's Day or when someone asked me to the prom, but nothing that extravagant. There had to be two-dozen roses in there, like I had won a pageant.

He knocked and I went to the door to open it. This was it, the possible beginning to my new present and distant future, or maybe neither one. Tonight was important either way.

The instant look of appreciation when he saw me made my heart flutter.

"You are breathtaking," he said, with a sense of awe in his voice.

"Thank you," I replied, not sure what else to say. Then I stepped back so he could come inside and once inside I informed him. "Momma is coming. She's getting my younger sister's started on making dinner. Then she'll be in here."

He was still looking at me. "I'm in no rush."

I kept waiting on him to hand me the roses. Was I supposed to offer to take them and put them in water? Perhaps I should yank them away? I've seen this happen in movies, though I wasn't sure what I should do. I thought the man handed the woman the flowers and then commented on her looks.

Momma walked into the room before I could decide and her attention went directly to Hale. He immediately responded, shifting his body, giving momma a respectful distance.

"Good evening, Marjaline Knox," she said, holding out her hand.

Hale took it in the hand that was free: "Hale Jude, ma'am." Then he handed the roses to her. "These are for you. A way to thank you for trusting me with your daughter this evening. It's obvious where she gets her looks from."

He was good at this. As cliché as that had sounded I think my mother blushed. Jude's attractiveness was hard to ignore. Even for a woman my mother's age. You simply had to look at the man.

"Thank you. I expect her home by eleven thirty. She's a good girl, Hale Jude. I want her to return that way."

He nodded. "Of course."

I, on the other hand, wanted to crawl under the table and hide. This sounded like a talk a mother would give a high school prom date. Not a grown man. I wasn't a child anymore.

"Well then, it's good to meet you," she said, then turned her attention to me. "Have a good time."

That was code for don't do anything stupid and be home when I said.

"Yes ma'am," I replied.

"Momma, Bessy won't let me eat a cookie!" Henry cried as he ran into the room. He saw Hale and froze, his eyes growing large, unaccustomed to a man being present.

"That's because it's almost dinner time. Get back in that

kitchen and set the table like I told you."

Henry responded "okay," his eyes never leaving Hale's. My brother backed away as if he alone knew something we didn't beforehand. Henry then turned to run. I would remember this happened later. Then it all went back to normal. "Gwirls! There's a man in yonder!"

I grinned and looked at Hale. He seemed rather amused. "That was Henry my little brother. He's cherished the cupcakes you bought."

Hale chuckled. "I'll have to remember to stop by the bakery more often."

Momma frowned at that. I wasn't sure if it was because the idea of Henry eating more sugar was a bad one, or that Hale smothering me was a bother. Either way I decided we needed to get out of there before Bessy made up a reason to come in the room or Milly got home from work.

"I'll see you tonight momma." I then turned to cue the leaving.

Hale followed and opened the door for me to go through first.

"Again, it was a pleasure meeting you," he told momma. She shook her head in response and then left.

Once we were safely outside I exhaled.

"You sound relieved." His tone was amused.

"Trust me. The worst part of the evening is over. With that I have abundant experience. We were lucky, fortunate and blessed."

He laughed. Thought it was funny. He didn't know I'd defused a bomb. Or how badly that could've gone.

Sixteen

I'M NOT SURE exactly what I expected. But this wasn't it. A burger joint on the Alabama-Tennessee line was definitely not what I had in mind when I thought about where Hale Christopher Jude III would take me on a date. The good thing was I wasn't over dressed. However, I guess maybe I thought a nice steak place would be his choice. Like, perhaps, All Steak in Cullman. I'd always heard how good it was and some of my friends had gone on dates there. When I was dressing this evening All Steak had been my hope, where I thought Hale would take me.

This place was not All Steak.

The expensive smell of leather in Hale's Mercedes put me in the mindset of country clubs and fancy things. Even if this was our only date I wanted the memory of what that felt like. The burger place had red plastic booths with linoleum tables that looked like they hadn't been updated since nineteen seventy. Records hung on the wall and Lean On Me played on the radio. He was giddy and happy to be here.

Hale further surprised me by ordering a cheeseburger with

fries. He didn't look like the kind of man to eat something so greasy. I went with the meatloaf because at places like this that was always the best thing on the menu. He took a sip of his soda, also something I hadn't imagined him drinking, Hale striking me as an expensive bourbon or brandy guy. Like the ones I read about in books.

"Are you planning on going to college?" he asked, leaning back in his cheap plastic seat that was faded from the sun on a corner.

"I . . . ," and then I stopped.

This was a line of questioning I hadn't expected. I figured he had some degree from a college that was private with ivy on the walls and with students who wore sweaters and caps. Hearing my honest answer wasn't going to impress him, but I wasn't one to lie.

"No. We can't afford that. Milly, my older sister, put herself through cosmetology school. She's a hair stylist now. But I don't much want to do that. I hate fixing my own hair much less someone else's. And there ain't a job for me that would pay full tuition, except maybe dancing on a pole, that would put me through in four years."

Hale laughed at that. Then he nodded his head. "Agreed, it would take a good paying job to get you through college."

In all honesty I had considered the dancing on a pole thing. Once. But I figured that wasn't for me. My momma would die of embarrassment and I just couldn't do that to her. Not to mention my daddy would roll over in his grave. I knew a girl who did it for a year. She flew off of the pole, helicoptered around, and took out the entire front row. Her tips that night came to $1,200 and she only fractured an ankle. That's a beautiful story.

"So your plan is what?" he asked me.

This was an even less impressive answer. Why couldn't we talk about something else? My future wasn't what I imagined us discussing. Maybe our taste in music or places we wanted to go?

In his case places he had been.

"I'll work at the bakery for now. Then one day the right opportunity will come along and I'll take it. Leave that town behind. Not sure how, but I will. For the moment though, I'll wait."

He fell silent. I took a drink of my sweet tea and wondered if my answer wasn't good enough. Even if I had to get another job to save money I would get out of Moulton.

"How long have you wanted to leave Moulton?"

"As long as I can remember," I replied. "Maybe longer."

He then leaned forward on the table. "I think I might have an idea. Something for you to consider. I don't expect a decision right away."

My heart began beating so hard in my chest I could hear it in my ears. An idea to get out of Moulton? I wanted to say "YES" right now, though I waited for him to continue, before agreeing to anything.

"I have a penthouse in Manhattan I mentioned before. My live in caretaker has retired from old age. It was too much for her to keep things up. I need someone to live there, to take care of the place, keep it clean and prepare it with food when I'm coming into town. Could be short notice and most of the time it is on the shortest of notice. I like things kept clean and tidy at all times. I don't allow employees to have visitors in my home. I don't like the intrusiveness of that. Otherwise, it's a simple job. Not very demanding unless I'm in town and choose to entertain a guest, which I often do you see." He paused and looked at me a moment. "Are you interested? It is in Manhattan. This would be an adventure."

Words wouldn't come. I lost them. This was not what I expected. With the cupcakes and flirting I actually thought he wanted to date me outright. But he'd been looking for something else. Though it was my way out of Moulton.

I glanced around the diner and then realized he had brought me here for a reason. So I wouldn't get the wrong idea. His interest in me and the plans for my future were because I had been on a job interview and hadn't known till now. This all made sense and I smirked. He was polished and refined. I wasn't. He couldn't invite me into his world as someone he was dating.

But this was the chance of a lifetime.

"The pay would be one thousand dollars a week plus room and board. You would buy the groceries on a credit card I give you and your meals would be covered. I also offer health insurance to all employees."

Holy crap! I only made eight hundred dollars a month now.

He was waiting for me to respond. To offer some sort of reply. All I could manage was a nod of my head because I was leveled with shock.

"That's a yes then?" he asked, a grin on his face and then I nodded again and quickly he asked the next one.

"Well then, how soon can you move?"

How soon could I move? Leave Moulton and move to Manhattan. Holy crap! Holy crap! Holy freaking crap! Was I dreaming? Did he lace the meatloaf? Frowning, I found the words. "Is this a dream? Are my organs going to be stolen? Will I be sold into sex slavery?"

His laughter grew and the way it made his eyes shine was beautiful and strangely dark. Hale had become my boss. Nothing more. He was hiring me to work in a place where he only visited briefly. I had to remember this.

"It's not a dream, Sam," he replied, surprising me by shortening my name. "This is very real. An opportunity."

I pinched myself just to be sure. The small sharp pain was a relief.

"This week. I can leave this week."

Seventeen

I WAS HOME an hour before momma said I should be. After our business dinner we drove back to my house and he walked me to the door then gave me his number, took mine and said he'd be in touch by Monday with my travel arrangements.

There was obviously no kiss and the whole flirty-interested vibe I'd gotten from him in our past meetings was completely gone. Now he was very professional and businesslike.

When I walked in the door I heard momma in the kitchen. She was normally in bed this time of the night. With my being out she wasn't going to sleep. After I told her about my new job I wondered if she would sleep at all. Actually, I wasn't sure how she was going to feel about this. Would she be happy that I was finding a way to see the world or upset about my leaving home, alone to New York City? Either way I was going. I just didn't want to upset her. I wanted her to be happy for me.

"He didn't ask me out because he's interested in me the way you think."

She folded the towel in her hands, placed it by the sink and then looked up at me. "Is that so?"

I nodded. "He wants to hire me as a housekeeper at his penthouse in Manhattan. He has several places all over the world and the lady he had working in this one retired. The pay is one thousand a week plus room, board, and health insurance."

There, I said it all.

Momma pulled out a chair from around the table and sank down with a weary sigh. "You're gonna go aren't you."

It wasn't a question. It was just acceptance. Minus any excitement.

"It's my way out, momma. My chance to live another life. I can save money and then maybe go to college or with this reference get another job when it's time. This is the means to that end. Without a man attached."

She shook her head. "That's where you're wrong. There is a man attached."

"Yes, but he's my boss. He took me to a diner momma. Nothing fancy. He talked business and explained that when he was in town he would entertain guests and I was to keep it clean and the food stocked. That was it. He also said he only came a few days a month."

"Is he married?" she asked me.

I shook my head. "No." Honestly, I wasn't sure. He didn't wear a ring, but did that mean anything?

"Does he have a girlfriend? Fiancé?"

"Possibly, probably, I don't know. We just talked about my job and that's it. He doesn't share his personal stuff with me."

Momma rubbed her hand over her face and for a moment we sat there, neither of us speaking. The reality that I was taking this job and leaving was settling in for us both.

"Reckon you're grown and I can't tell you any different. You want out of this place and this is a ticket out. But remember these words: ain't no man hires a girl with your looks to just clean his house and cook. He'll want more. Maybe not now, but he will. And you'll have to make that decision. Just know that this here is home and when you need to run back the door is always open."

This was home. The girls, even though they could drive me nuts, were a part of me forever. And Henry was my heart. I would miss them all. Especially momma. But living with security, and always sense, wasn't the way to chase your dreams. Dreams were scary. This was supposed to be scary.

"I know momma."

She nodded her head, released a sigh and stood on weary legs. "Since you were a little girl I knew you'd be the one to leave me. That face has stopped traffic and brought attention all your life. You don't see it or feel it, but Mr. Hale does. Don't forget that. He's a man and you're beautiful. Inside and out. Don't let that ever change Sammy Jo."

I stood to close the distance between us. Tears stung my eyes and momma wrapped me in her arms. "I love you," I told her, as the first tear rolled down my cheek.

"And I love you."

We stood like that for a long time. My future playing out in our heads, imagining what it would be like in New York City really soon. How my life would change and I would adjust. I knew momma was full of concerns and fears. I'd call her weekly and keep her updated. After a while she wouldn't worry. She'd see I was able to handle it, was going to be okay.

She believed Hale was attracted to my beauty. Momma didn't realize there were beautiful women with class and money all around him. He could date models and heiresses. I wasn't the prettiest girl in the world. Though convincing my momma of that was impossible. So I let it go. I knew this was a business agreement.

My attraction to Hale would fade with time or at least I hoped it would. I didn't need to be attracted to my boss. That would lead to heartache. In Manhattan I wouldn't stand out like I apparently did in Moulton. There would be beauty and wealth all around me. I would be nothing else but me. I looked forward to that.

But I was going to miss this house. My momma, sisters, brother, Jamie, Ben and even the bakery, were all a part of me. The largest slice of what I was and in the future would become. This place had built me from the ground up and now I'd leave it behind. Instead of dancing around in joy I felt sad and anxious in leaving. Because I knew I would miss it all. Staying here was out of the question. I wanted more and had to go get it.

Knowing I could always come home again was what eased my ache and gave me the courage to do this from the start. I wasn't running away. I was only going forward. To a life that was worth writing about and maybe I'd do that too. Write about this. Document my journey. Share it one day with my kids. I'd make a mark on this world and in return, this world would mark me too. I'd clutch on with both hands and enjoy the ride and see what happened in time. Daddy always said it wasn't the destination, but the journey, that's what mattered. My journey was about to begin. Or had it begun already?

Eighteen

WHEN I FIRST told my sisters they were all giddy with excitement and hopes for a visit. Once packing began things changed. It was Bessy who cracked first. She walked into the bedroom where I was putting my clothes into the only suitcase we owned. Momma had been given the suitcase as a wedding gift from her mother. We haven't had a reason to use it since my mother was married. Seeing it packed was too much on Bessy and her tears weren't quiet ones. Within seconds she was sobbing loudly, in a heap on the floor in hysterics. I stopped and went to sit beside Bessy, pulling her into my arms.

"I ca-ca-can't imagine," she said with a sob, "life without you here." Honestly, neither could I.

"I won't be gone forever. I'll come visit and bring presents from New York. I will call every week and you can call me. Just think of the stories and adventures I'll get to tell you about."

She clung to me and continued to cry. All I could do was hold her. Eventually Henry walked into the room followed by Hazel and when Hazel saw us tears welled up in her eyes. She knew why Bessy was crying, even if Henry was confused. The idea of me moving was so foreign to him he wasn't sure what to think.

"I'll come home for the holidays with presents and we will talk about all I've missed. Maybe one day you can come visit me. I'll save up so you can." I tried those encouraging words, though nothing eased them entirely. While we sat piled in the floor as a family I let them cry it out.

Henry came to sit in my lap and laid his head on my chest. I wasn't sure how long we sat there. I did not rush their sadness. When the tears dried we waited in the silence. I would miss them. That was felt. I'd hold onto this moment forever. Not because of sadness, but because we were family and that bond is never severed, even if we wished it to be.

Jamie's tears hadn't been much better. She was emotional and pregnant so I spent two hours consoling her like a mother. If I ever wondered how much these people loved me, I definitely knew it now. To me, that meant the world.

It was Sunday morning when I got the call from Hale's personal assistant. Felicity was her name. She was emailing me my flight information and the list of travel details. I was to fly out of Nashville at eight on Monday, the move happening rapidly as my questions increased by the second and by the minute.

Felicity assured me that all of the answers were contained within my email. I explained I didn't have an email account and she asked if I had any access. I told her I did because Jamie had a laptop with an Internet connection. She then gave me a website, login name and a password all my own. I apparently had one now.

After getting my information printed off at Jamie's I took it to momma for perusing. She read it and said we would leave the house at four the next morning and that I needed to be packed and have my driver's license with me.

Sleep didn't come easily. I was too nervous and anxious. I

kept reading over the details Felicity had sent me in the email. I would be here and then I'd be there. Things changing rather quickly, which is exactly as I wished, though still, this was hard. Here were the particulars as follows:

```
8:00am
Nashville to Atlanta
Nashville Intl. (BNA) to Hartsfield-Jackson Atlanta
Intl. (ATL)
Delta 496
Seat 3A
BOEING (DOUGLAS) MD-88
Layover
1h 58m stop Atlanta (ATL)
12:10p
Atlanta to New York
Hartsfield-Jackson Atlanta Intl. (ATL) to John F.
Kennedy Intl. (JFK)
Delta 1415
Seat 4D
```

```
Arrival at JFK:
Upon arrival you will proceed to baggage claim.
Your driver will be waiting with a sign that has
your name on it. He will get your luggage and take
you to the penthouse. Once there the details of
your job and instructions will be on the kitchen
counter. The key, credit card, and keyless entry
code will also be waiting on you. Once you have
gone over everything sign the contract and fax it
to me from the fax machine in the office down the
hall to your left. My number will be listed if you
have any questions.
```

```
    Safe travels,
    Felicity
```

I read over it a million times to be sure I wasn't missing

something. The fear that I would do the wrong thing and end up somewhere lost was real and apparent to me. I had never been on a plane. I had barely been out of Moulton.

Finally I folded the paper and tucked it back in my purse. Then I rolled over to look at Hazel who was sound asleep beside me. She would grow so much this year. She was already beautiful, but this year, Hazel would really blossom. I felt a touch of sadness over missing that, but yes, I would miss it.

Leaving had always been my dream. Now hours before I actually left I was torn between wanting to hold onto here and going to chase my new life. I wanted both, but couldn't live two. I had to choose and I'd chosen.

Closing my eyes I let myself dream of how New York City would look and the places I would explore. The new friends I would find and the future I wanted were right there for the taking. Leaving my past behind wasn't a permanent thing. I could always come visit I thought.

Tomorrow, I would finally grow up.

Nineteen

MOMMA HADN'T CRIED. That was the one thing I was most thankful for today. After very little sleep if she had cried it would have been so much worse. I was on the verge of tears leaving my room behind. All my sisters were sleeping as I eased out with my suitcase. I hadn't wanted to wake them for fear of becoming emotional and again, the pile of us crying. Yet, I wanted to hug them all one last time.

Henry, on the other hand, sleeps like a rock so I was able to go kiss his little head and whisper I love you to him before leaving. He didn't stir once. The sound of the screen door closing behind me as we stepped outside was sad. I knew I wouldn't hear it again, at least for a while anyway.

The rest of my day had taken my complete concentration in order not to miss my connecting flight. For someone who had never flown before the Atlanta airport was confusing. I stopped to ask for help three times before I figured out that I needed to get on this indoor train thing and go from letter A to letter C. Then look for gate 19.

I was fed on my flight from Atlanta to New York and even given a real cloth napkin for my lap. The glass with my soda in it was real, not plastic, like I had imagined. When I went to the restroom I realized there was a curtain separating my small section of the plane with the rest of the passengers. Looking around at the suits and laptops surrounding me I realized this wasn't the normal part of the plane. Hale had put me in a special section.

My flowered sundress and sandals, which felt pretty yesterday as I spent hours deciding what to wear, now felt as if they were bought from a thrift store. They hadn't been. I bought them on sale at the local department store last year and was, as recently as before I boarded this plane, quite proud of them.

By the time I arrived at JFK airport I was mentally exhausted from thinking too much. I felt alone and scared. However, while stepping off the plane and making my way to the baggage claim by following the signs, excitement began to grow with each second. I was doing it. I was in New York.

Tonight, at this very moment, I would've been in Moulton listening to the same gossip I always heard. I wouldn't be getting up in the morning and going to the bakery. No more canning this summer. No tripping to the lake with the people from my childhood who had known me since I could remember. That was finished. I was here. It was happening.

My life was going to be in full color. Change was happening now and I was present for the change.

A man holding a sign with my name on it, like Felicity said he would be, was waiting on me near the baggage. He was in a black suit and tie, his head bald and he stood amongst a sea of men dressed the same way as I entered the baggage claim area. Her directions had been easy to follow. I was thankful for the paper in my purse. Appreciative of her instructions. Their step-by-step delivery.

I walked up to the man and smiled. "I'm Sam Knox," I told him. The fact my sign hadn't said Sammy Jo didn't surprise me. Hale didn't call me that. Or at least he had stopped. He preferred to shorten it.

The older man smiled. "Welcome to New York," he replied, placing the sign under his arm. "Let's get your luggage shall we."

I followed him until he stopped at a carousel with luggage moving on it. We passed three before he halted. I was trying to figure out how he knew which one my luggage would arrive on. The one thing I was sure he didn't know was which piece of luggage was mine. So I turned my attention to the moving bags until I spotted my piece. "There's mine," I said, stepping up to get it.

"I'll get that miss," he replied, moving in front of me and picking the bag up as he came by.

That was nice of him. My momma would approve. We might not be in the south, but so far I didn't see a difference in the people here. They were all very helpful and nice.

"Thank you," I told him.

He smiled. "Of course. Follow me."

He carried my suitcase toward the exit doors and I did as he said. The air was warm. It was summer, but being from the south I assumed it never got this hot up north. I realized I was incorrect. The sun was beaming down and I was thankful for my sundress. We didn't walk far before he stopped beside a black sedan that was sleek and expensive looking. I watched as he opened the back door and waved his hand at me with a smile. "Please make yourself comfortable. The water in the cup holder is chilled and the mints are also for your enjoyment."

I felt like I was on the plane again. Being catered to. This was not something I was accustomed to hearing or receiving except in dreams or hallucinations, after drinking too much punch. And since I was being hired as a housekeeper it seemed odd I would be traveling this way.

"Thank you," I paused, realizing I didn't even know his name. "I'm sorry, I don't believe I got your name."

He looked like he might chuckle, but instead he replied "Williams. Miss, you can call me Williams."

That was an odd first name. I then returned his smile. "Thank you Williams. You've made my arrival here very easy and welcoming."

"My pleasure, miss."

I liked Williams. He would do well in Moulton. Not that he'd ever want to leave the excitement of New York for Moulton, but still, I could see him there. He was a helpful, nice and considerate man and I didn't at all feel like the big city would murder or rape me, which a lot of small town people often do.

I climbed inside and picked up the water bottle that was shaped in an odd square. The ice cold plastic felt good after a walk in the heat and I opened it and took a long drink. I didn't reach for a mint, instead watching out the window as Williams got into the driver's seat and we began to move. The airport parking lot was new and amazing with hundreds of people bustling about and I wondered if anyone famous was close without me noticing.

"It's a thirty minute drive in the traffic. This time of the day it is. I'll have you to the penthouse as soon as I can and I apologize for the delay."

"Okay," I replied. "Lordy, you're precious. I ain't special in the least." I was happy to be able to just sit back and take it all in in gulps. The streets were what you'd expect, busy and pulsing with life. It was almost fifteen minutes before we went through a tunnel, emerging into what I imagined New York City would look like.

We were actually here. This was it. I had arrived.

My fingers knotted into fists and the grin on my face spread wide from cheek to cheek. Moulton was behind me and this new world was building itself around me. I couldn't wait to explore it.

Twenty

HE BUILDING WAS historical and the curve of its front came to a point at the street. More like points, it was amazing. I stood outside it, taking in the swarms of people around me in movement, gazing up at the place that would be my home and I couldn't see the roof in the least. I'd always been able to see it. In Moulton one saw roofs.

"Mr. Jude's penthouse is located at the top in the curve. You'll like that," Williams said as he walked up behind me carrying my luggage. "Come with me."

I tore my eyes from the structure and like a child hurried behind him inside. Williams had to punch in a code to get us further than that. A man in a suit was standing at the door and Williams introduced me: "this is Miss Samantha Knox. She will be living in Mr. Jude's penthouse." The man nodded and stepped back for us to go forward. Once we got to the bank of elevators I was thankful that Williams wasn't leaving. I couldn't figure this out alone. My hands were shaking, from excitement or fear, which one I wasn't sure. The unknown was all around me.

We stopped on the eleventh floor and the doors opened. A long hallway led to a set of double doors and Williams looked to me. "You should have the code to the keyless entry in your instructions miss."

Oh. Yes I did.

Quickly I got out the paper that Jamie had printed for me and scanned to the bottom. The numbers 382650 were waiting there for me. I located and looked at the door's keypad and then I asked William's a question.

"I just put this number in here?"

"Yes miss," was his response.

So I did. Punched it carefully.

Like magic the lock slid away with a click and I opened the door for the first time. The view was instantaneous. Forgetting to walk inside I stood there and took it all in. What I could see from the doorway. The entryway alone was bigger than my house in Moulton, maybe double.

"Would you like to go in?" Williams asked me.

I snapped out of my daze and stepped inside so he could follow and set my bag down.

"This is where I leave you mam. If you have any questions just call Felicity. She's a real pro at her job."

I wanted to ask William's to stay. He was the only person I knew in this city of over eight million people, not counting tourists and whatnot, though I couldn't restrain the driver. He had a job, other people to pick up.

"Thank you so much Williams. You've been great."

He nodded, turned and left me. Closing the double doors behind him. I moved to lock them, but the slide on its own, made its familiar click. I realized it did that internally.

Turning back to my new home I began to smile, then laughed

until I cried. This was real, I was here, experiencing this and it had all happened in a week. I left my suitcase where Williams had placed it and walked over to the full-length windows. Floor to ceiling, a first for me. They lined what looked like a living room area and I tell you the view was amazing. I wanted to sleep right here. Wake up to this view every morning.

If my sisters could see this they would pass out. Bessy would lose her mind. If I had a camera I would take photos and send them home every week. But that was something I never saved up for. I guess they cost lots of dollars.

There was a list on the counter in the kitchen for me. I made my way through into the next room and found an all white kitchen, with equally beautiful views. The only color in the kitchen was the black marble counters and the amber light fixtures on the ceiling. There was a fresh arrangement of flowers sitting in the middle of the island. Beside it was a sheet of paper. I walked over and picked it up, finding what Felicity had promised. Everything I needed to know. Beside it was an envelope. I found a black American Express card with my name embossed across it. There was a stack of one hundred dollar bills that weren't Monopoly money. I dropped both of them directly back onto the counter like they were on fire or something. Then I went back to my note. Surely there was an explanation.

I knew I'd have a card, but my name was on this one, and the cash was without reason. I quickly read her letter, looking up only briefly, to see what she was talking about. I glanced toward the white swinging door that led to another section. I figured the first door on the right was meant to be my room.

The money was mine. My first weeks pay. I picked it up and counted the hundred dollar bills because the man was paying me in cash. I found that odd, but I didn't argue. I assumed I would be responsible for my taxes. Since he wasn't cutting them out. I'd need to ask Felicity about that. I had no idea how that worked.

The card was for the needs of the penthouse. It was in my name to make it easier for me to use in the stores. They could also keep a better record on what I spent for the place. That made sense to me. I wouldn't go on any wild sprees. Didn't want to party down in the penthouse.

Once I was sure I knew everything I should do today, I slowly walked towards the door, to enter the room that was mine.

"Holy, mother of pearl!"

Again, it was all white. With the exception of a tan chair and ottoman sleekly sitting in the corner. Some paintings with a charcoal grey were hanging perfectly centered on the wall. The blanket on the corner of the bed was the same color as the paintings. Other than that it was all very white, the views from the three windows overlooking the busy city. This was a different side of the building from the one I had previously viewed. I stood taking in everything below me, as if that world couldn't touch me.

The note said there was a grocery store two blocks west of here. I would go and find that next. Felicity had listed a few local deli's and bakery's she thought I'd enjoy. I appreciated her help.

There was also a library in this very building and a spa for tenants and guests. I wanted to go find them both. They had a basketball court, of which I had no interest, though it was nice to know they had one. I headed back down the hall to the entry onto the balcony. Felicity said there were plants to water outside the penthouse.

As I stepped into the open it wasn't like the balcony of a penthouse in New York City. It was similar to an English garden. There were plants and flowers everywhere. Lounging furniture that looked so comfortable one could sleep on it like a bed. The only way you would know it wasn't a garden was to walk over to the edge and look at the view below you. It was like having the best of both worlds. I didn't know why Hale would ever leave, for it was all I'd dreamed about.

Twenty-One

FINDING THE GROCERY store had been a little difficult simply because it didn't look like what I imagined. It was a storefront and the food selection was nothing like the Piggly Wiggly we had back home. But eventually I found it and stocked the kitchen with food I wanted along with the food on Felicity's list.

After putting things away and finding there was nothing for me to clean as of yet, I poured myself a glass of sweet tea and went out on the balcony to watch the city and relax. Believing this to be real was hard. I wanted to share it with someone, though that was the drawback here. I was alone and personally sharing, would be with myself for now.

Sleep came easy and deep. My lack of rest from the night before caught up with me and I fell asleep quickly. Sunlight streaming in the window the next morning woke me. That, and the sound of the city. So different than the silence of the country life I had grown accustomed to hearing. Or rather, not hearing at all.

I wondered if I would be able to sleep as easily with the

noise tonight. When I wasn't exhausted from travel. Stretching, I got up, made my bed and went to the kitchen, to make myself some breakfast.

Then, what would I do? I had nothing to clean and no further instructions from Felicity on the matter. I was in this big city with no one. With the chance I'd been hoping for. I didn't need someone else to explore. I could do that on my own. Besides, I had money. I could visit museums, take a cab to Central Park and then go and see Times Square.

Excited about seeing things I'd only seen on television, I quickly ate the cereal I bought yesterday, then went to get dressed for my outing. Eventually I would have real work to do. When Hale came into town and had guests to entertain. For now I could enjoy the life I'd been offered. Tonight I'd call momma, my sisters and Henry and tell them all about my day. Everything I saw and the people I met. I knew momma would want to hear from me, to make sure that I arrived safely. She didn't seem crushed when I left her, but I knew the reason for that. I think my mother wants more for me. More than the hand she'd been dealt.

I was almost dressed to leave when the phone began to ring. I turned and searched for the sound and eventually found it in the foyer. It wasn't a regular phone. It was a fancy touch screen device. Thanks to Jamie I knew how this worked and quickly answered the call. The name "Felicity" was on the screen so I knew who was going to speak.

"Hello," I said quickly, somewhat afraid that it rang too many times.

"Good, you've found the phone. I forgot to leave instructions about it, seeing as it was a hurried addition and Mr. Jude forgot to mention it. The phone has my number, Mr. Jude's number, your home number and a few numbers for food delivery available in that area that are highly recommended. Feel free to add whomever else you want. Mr. Jude will arrive tomorrow at noon. Be sure to have the foods from his list and freshen up and prepare his room as described on the notes I left you. He will be alone this time so there is no need to become invisible. Do you have any questions?"

"Uh, no, I understand."

"Good, call if you need anything. Goodbye Samantha," she said, then abruptly ended the call.

Samantha? Did she think that was what Sam was short for? Frowning, I set the phone down and quickly picked it back up and slipped it into the pocket of my jean shorts. In case she called back.

Sightseeing wasn't happening today. I headed to the kitchen to go over the instructions for Hale's arrival. I hadn't expected him so soon. I was happy he was coming and that I wouldn't be alone. There would be someone in this city that I knew.

The idea of having drinks and watching the city sky with Hale made me smile. I shouldn't think about him other than as my boss. But the man was fascinating. And I had so many questions I wanted to ask him. About the city and the world in general.

I could call momma later. On my new cellular phone. A job perk I hadn't expected. This meant I had a camera now. When I did get to take that sightseeing outing I could snap photos like a lunatic.

A musical sound startled me and I stood there looking around the room. It took a moment for me to figure out it was a doorbell. We didn't have a doorbell at home. Much less one that played a classical tune. I couldn't imagine who could be here. But I went to the door anyway.

The man standing on the other side was what one might call sexy. Or alluring, things like that. There were no other words for him. He wasn't polished and expensive like Hale. He was, ahh, an anti-Hale. Gorgeous with dark hair and big blue eyes, his torn jeans worn at the bends. The boots he had on were for actual labor and that body of his had worked.

"Is Hale in?" he asked, studying me as closely as I was studying him.

"No," I said, feeling my cheeks heat and redden from looking at him. I really liked his boots. And the tight black tee shirt he was wearing. "He arrives tomorrow."

The man seemed annoyed by this answer. "And you are?"

"Sammy Jo Knox, the new housekeeper," I replied. I felt the need to defend my presence. This wasn't Moulton, Alabama.

He began to twist his mouth, a smirk then touching his lips. "Sure you are. The bastard," he muttered under his breath.

I didn't know what that meant exactly. I was deciding that Mr. Cowboy Texas, straight out of a romance novel, was someone I didn't like.

"Can I help you?" I asked in the coolest business tone I could muster. I wasn't real big on sounding professional.

"Probably not sugar. Probably not."

Well, fine then. "Hale will be here tomorrow at noon if you'd like to return then." I had the urge to slam the door in his face but seeing as this could be a friend or business relation of Hale's I didn't do it that instant.

"Tell him Ezra stopped by. We need to talk."

Ezra. What an odd name for a cowboy. Unless he jumped out of birthday cakes, dancing around naked and whatnot.

"Okay."

He turned to leave, then glanced back. "Be careful sugar. Ain't much here for you. Don't ever let your guard down. Here's not what you're used to."

I didn't respond to that. I firmly closed the door. Then I stuck out my tongue and growled in frustration. He'd said "ain't" and "sugar." He might as well be from Alabama. Sure wasn't from here I can tell you. The asshole. Judging me because of the way

I talked or looked. I didn't need his advice or opinion.

If I were lucky I'd never lay eyes on Ezra again in this city. Or any other place on earth.

Twenty-Two

ONCE I STARTED cleaning and straightening for Hale's arrival I began to find more things to do. I put fresh sheets on his bed and fluffed the thick luxurious towels in his bathroom. I went and bought flowers from the street vender I'd passed yesterday and put them in the empty vase by his bed. I wanted to be good at this.

He was giving me a chance to live and I didn't want to give him something to complain about. I bought everything on his list and used the delivery number for the wine he requested. Felicity said they had his information on file and wouldn't card me. They'd just leave it downstairs at reception and I could pick it up there.

I made sure all the wine glasses were clear of spots from the dishwasher and then went about dusting, although there wasn't any dust. Then I watered the plants outside. In a few I put ice cubes instead. I wasn't sure what that was all about, but I did as I was instructed.

The day went by quickly and I had no more calls or visitors stopping by. I was glad for that. I was finishing up dinner when I decided it was a good time to call home and speak with momma. As much as being here and walking outside were exciting, I still missed home. I wouldn't go back but they were my people, before here the only life I knew.

After the delivery of the wine I racked it, then took my new phone and called.

At the sound of Bessy's voice saying "hello" tears stung my eyes.

"It's me Bessy," I said, smiling as I sat down on the sofa.

"Sammy Jo?" she asked, with excitement in her voice.

"Yes, I have a new phone number so y'all can get in touch with me. How are things at home?"

"The same. How are things in New York!"

"Definitely not the same. I've been working since I got here so I haven't seen much, but the view from the balcony is amazing. It's just like what you've seen on the television set and in the movies, all of the movies. I feel like I'm in one walking these streets. I had to go to the grocery and shop. That was its own adventure."

"I wish you could send pictures," she said.

"I can! Soon. My new work phone is one of those smart phones with a camera."

"Oh wow, wow Sammy Jo. You're living the life I bet."

"I want to talk to Sammy Jo," Hazel said from the background.

"Give me the phone," Momma then added.

"We'll talk soon! Here's momma."

"Bye," I said to her. Hearing her voice had been good. Just what I needed to calm me.

"It's about time you called," momma said. "You arrived safely I take it?"

"Yes ma'am. It was an easy flight." I assured her instead of telling her how complicated finding the gates were at the airport.

"And how's this place you're living? Safe?"

"Safer than Moulton. You have to have a code to get in the doors downstairs. There's also a security guard. If he doesn't know you then you don't make it to the elevators."

"Good, good, and the neighborhood?"

"It's nice. Big. But the people here are nice. Nothing scary when I go out. I had to go to the grocery and shop. It was close and I was more amazed by the walk, than anything else in the store."

Momma sighed and it was relief.

"Met any of your neighbors?"

I wasn't sure if Ezra was a neighbor or not. But even if he was there was nothing to talk about. I didn't care for the man.

"No, but I've been working on the list of things left here for me to do. You wouldn't believe the garden on the balcony outside. I have to water the plants daily."

I was going to tell her that Hale was coming tomorrow but something stopped me. I didn't think she'd be okay with that. She would read more into it than there actually was.

"Well, alright then. It's good to hear your voice. Hazel wants to talk at you. Give me that number I can reach you at before I cut you loose."

I found the paper where I'd written it down and slowly repeated the digits.

"Love you, girl," momma said, before handing the phone to Hazel.

"Love you too momma," I replied.

"Sammy Jo! What's it like there? Have you seen movie stars?" Hazel asked almost immediately.

Laughing I leaned back on the sofa. She fired one question after another and I tried to answer them all. Leaving her in bed had been hard. I'd wanted to wake her and tell her goodbye and that I loved her then and forever. Hearing her voice now was just what I needed to soothe me.

"I talk to Sammy Jo," Henry kept demanding in the background. I could see them sitting around in the kitchen while momma made dinner for the bunch. Everyone was talking and working. Milly wouldn't be home yet. They'd eat dinner then clean up together while momma gave Henry his bath, before putting him to bed with a story. After they all had their baths they'd sit on their beds and talk about the day, Milly's date, who she saw at the salon, and who was dating or not.

As if Hazel could read my mind she said, "Jamie called today for your mailing address. They're sending out wedding invitations. She said she knew you couldn't make it back, but she wanted you to have an invitation."

"Thank you. I'll call Jamie and chat with her tonight."

"Can't believe she's getting married so young. I'm not doing that. I'm gonna travel the world like you."

Of all my sisters I believed Hazel would. The others would stay in Moulton, their entire lives lived there. But Hazel, she'd escape. Because she wanted to leave so badly.

Twenty-Three

ALTHOUGH I SLEPT well enough through the night with the noise outside, my eyes opened early. I was nervous about Hale's arrival. I didn't want to mess anything up. He hadn't called or texted and neither had Felicity to give me any new details. I showered and dressed then walked around looking for things to clean.

Walking in from the balcony there was a click at the door. I could hear more than one man's voice and I realized Hale wasn't alone. Did I hide if he was with someone or do I offer them drinks? Dang it, Felicity hadn't told me what to do in this situation.

The door swung open and Hale entered followed by Ezra. Great. Just the man I wanted to see again. No. Not. Ever.

"Come in and have some lunch. We can discuss your issues with the deal over a glass of wine. I need a break after that early morning flight. I don't want to deal with this as soon as I arrive." Hale spoke to Ezra as if they were old friends. His gaze then swung to me as he surveyed how I was dressed. His look of displeasure told me I had done something wrong.

"Hello, Samantha. You've already met Ezra. He'll be joining me for lunch."

Two things about that: he called me Samantha knowing my name was Sammy Jo. Then he spoke to me as if I knew what they were having for lunch. There was something on the list from Felicity about this. I needed to run to the kitchen and check that.

"Okay. Do you need anything at the moment? Or do you want me to go get lunch ready?"

He motioned for Ezra to go out to the balcony. "Bring us both a glass of the Sassicaia. Then you can start on lunch," he informed me.

I recognized the name and knew he was speaking about the wine. The problem was I'd never opened a bottle before. I wasn't sure how. These weren't screw top bottles.

"I need to check something Ezra. I'll meet you outside," he said, turning and heading for the kitchen.

I quickly followed, glad that we were going to be out of earshot from Ezra. I didn't need him to hear that I couldn't open a wine bottle.

Hale walked over to the wine rack and withdrew a bottle of the wine he had mentioned. "From the look on your face you have no idea how to open a bottle of wine. I'm going to show you and I want you to watch carefully. You'll need to be able to do this."

I nodded. "Of course."

He opened a drawer and pulled out a large black and metal contraption. I watched as he aligned the pointy tip of the screw over the cork then turned the top to twist it in. Lastly, he pushed the two sides down that had risen like wings and the cork came out with an easy pop.

I wanted to sigh in relief. I thought it was going to be much harder than that. "Okay, I can do that," I assured him.

He sat the contraption down then looked at me. "You

should've shopped for clothing yesterday. Your clothes are not going to be acceptable."

I hadn't known about clothing. Was that why he paid me early? To buy new clothes?

"I'm sorry. I wasn't aware I was supposed to use the money left for clothing."

Hale frowned. "Felicity didn't explain that?"

I liked Felicity. She was very good at her job so telling him "no, she hadn't," felt like ratting her out. "I'm, uh, sure she did and I missed it somewhere."

"Use the card. I'll leave a list of stores for you to shop at to buy a new wardrobe. The clothing you brought doesn't need to leave your suitcase. My world expects different. Understand?"

I nodded because I was beginning to understand. He had changed my name and now he was changing my clothing. But then, I thought, I am his employee and I need to look a certain way. I should accept that and not get so annoyed.

The words "yes sir" almost came out of my mouth.

"Good," then his face softened and he smiled. That sexy sweet smile that I remembered from the days he bought me cupcakes. He walked over to me and his hand cupped my cheek. It seemed intimate and I froze, startled by the touch.

"I like having you here when I arrive. I missed you," he said, with a tenderness he hadn't used with me before.

My stomach fluttered and I wasn't sure how to respond.

"Ezra will be here for a few hours. Less, if I'm lucky. We'll go shopping together if you'd like."

The idea of shopping with Hale frightened me. I wasn't going to know what kind of clothing he expected me to buy and the pressure of having him watch and study me didn't sound fun at all.

"You wear your thoughts so clearly in those eyes," he chuckled. "It's okay Sam. I'll help you shop."

I simply nodded. His hand fell away and my face still held the warmth of his touch. "I'll take the wine out. You can go ahead and start on lunch. If I were alone I'd have you join me, but Ezra is a business partner and I'll need some privacy."

I frowned. What kind of business partner could he be? "He doesn't look like you or your world," I said without thinking.

"He's from Texas," Hale replied, as if that explained it all.

"He's also rude and seems rough."

Hale laughed as he lifted the two glasses of wine. There was a drip from the bottle and his pour had been off center, though he had found the drop and thumbed it. The kitchen was perfect again. "He is. That's why he's good at his job."

I didn't say anything else, watching as Hale left the kitchen.

I had to figure out what lunch was. I knew the list of groceries Felicity sent said something about meal preparation. I knew how to cook just fine, but I was concerned that the fancy food Hale would request might be difficult to make. Instead of walking around cleaning all morning I should've been going over food and putting a menu together. Lesson learned. Next time I'd know.

Luckily there was a lunch example Felicity sent to prepare me in case of an emergency. Fresh crab with an Asian salad, their cost combined like buying a calf, but of course this was New York City. I fixed a plate with both of these, adding a side plate of hummus with pita chips and a mixture of vegetables. This was one of Hale's "go to meals." I felt safe serving them this.

She said to "take out the hummus first." This was an appetizer.

I wished I didn't have to see Ezra. I'd have to get over my aversion to him, sooner better than later.

Twenty-Four

ALE AND EZRA paused their conversation every time I delivered something. Hale lifted his empty wine glass. His way of telling me they needed refills. Momma would've slapped his face. Things in this world were different. More formal, and way less friendly.

Fortunately, Hale didn't look at me oddly when I served their courses of food. I suppose I was doing it correctly. I had to look at the bright side of this. At least I wasn't bored. Him being in town gave me something to do. And besides that was my job.

I kept busy in the kitchen cleaning and deciding what dinner would be. I wish Felicity had sent me a cookbook. That would have made things easier. The stuff I knew how to cook wasn't the food he wanted. Smiling, I thought about frying up some chicken with a pot of mashed potatoes and maybe some collard greens. That would be hilarious.

The kitchen door opened behind me. I put the last dish away and spoke: "I was about to come check and see if you needed anything more." Then I turned around.

It wasn't Hale. It was Ezra.

"Do you need something?" I asked. I tried not to sound annoyed.

He seemed amused by my tone, did a little head tilt, his blue eyes assessing intention. "No, but you may, eventually. Call me when that day comes."

What in the world? I started to ask him what he meant when he turned and left the kitchen. I heard him talking with Hale, followed by their laughter, then the door closing behind him. I considered telling Hale what he'd said, but then decided against it. I was not here for drama. Whatever Ezra meant by that was obviously not important. He hadn't even left me his number.

I turned off the kitchen lights and walked into the living room. Hale was standing at the window with an inch of wine staring out at the city. The view was spectacular and I hated to interrupt him. He had traveled all morning, went directly to a meeting and had to be nearly frazzled.

"You did well," he said, glancing back.

"Thank you."

"We have to get you better clothes. I wish you'd done that already. I expected a few issues to surface."

A few issues? He was acting like I was a disobedient child. That was unfair, but I kept my mouth shut, being patient and understanding.

"Ezra enjoyed lunch. That's really all that matters." His gaze traveled up and down me. "Is that the best outfit you brought?" He asked with the slightest of grimace.

I reminded myself not to take offense. Which was hard because I had a temper and my mouth would lash like a whip. Curbing it wasn't easy.

"No, I have a blue sundress that momma made me last year."

He did a slight lift of his shoulders. "I have a meeting at three.

We won't have time to shop for your clothing. You're a size four, am I right?"

I nodded yes, surprised he guessed so easily, by simply looking at me.

"I'll have some clothes sent for you. I won't be home for dinner tonight. Of course, feed yourself. But consider the rest of the day a break. Tomorrow we'll do something. What is it you want to see most?"

That was a hard choice. Fifth Avenue, Times Square and Central Park were all tied for first. I could visit the two that would take the longest when Hale was gone on business. I then replied "Times Square."

"Of course. We'll go see it tomorrow. Then I'll take you to one of my favorite lunch spots."

That sounded fun. I was ready to explore the city. Having someone with me would be nice.

"Until your clothes arrive go change into the blue dress." He said it with a wave of his hand as if I were being dismissed. He then turned his attention back to the city and the view outside the window.

Hale confused me. He could be so nice and make me feel wanted then treat me as if I were a child needing instruction and guidance. I wasn't sure how to feel about that, but I reminded myself he had given me this job and a chance to see the world. I was living in a penthouse in New York City. This was better than what I'd expected. Though I really didn't know what that was. I could learn to understand Hale. He was just different, that's all. What I knew were the people from Moulton, Alabama and it was me that needed to adjust. Not Hale. He was himself. I was the one that needed to change.

I went to my room and undressed. The blue Easter sundress that momma had made hanging in the closet to my front. I slipped it on and straightened it out. It was the nicest thing I owned, yet here it seemed inadequate. Country. That's what I was. Country. I didn't want to be. My place of birth wasn't my choice. I longed to be a part of this city, to fit in and not stand out.

Sitting down on the edge of the bed I looked out the windows of my room. Imagined what I might be like if I'd grown up in New York City. Would I speak differently? Walk with more confidence? Would my vocabulary be more extensive? Would I know the difference between fresh mozzarella and Brie, which confused me at the grocery store, just like the damn airport gates.

But had I been raised here I wouldn't have momma, my sisters or Henry or the memories of my daddy, and Jamie and Ben would be strangers. And I wanted all of them in my life. Being raised in Moulton wasn't what I hated. It was the idea of being stuck there for life. I'd gotten out and now I could truly appreciate my raising and my normal childhood.

A knock at my door startled me awake. Then it opened and Hale walked in. He took in my dress without smiling. "Your new clothing will arrive this evening. I know females like to shop for themselves and you will get a chance to do that. I'll go with you when you do. But for now you need appropriate clothing. I should've seen to that myself."

Again, with my clothes. Lord Jesus! They weren't as bad as he was carrying on. I bit my tongue to keep from saying just that and my thoughts must have shown on my face because he gave me an apologetic smile. "Soon you'll be ready to go out with me. You can attend dinners, like the one tonight, alongside me when properly dressed. We have to polish you up. Your beauty is enough to distract a man, but the women in this world can be brutal. They will pick you apart and eat you."

Go with him? Why? Although the idea of a fancy party in New York was exciting I wasn't sure why I would go along too.

"You want to take me to dinners with you?" I was tired of keeping my mouth shut. Sometimes I needed answers.

He grinned and walked over to stand in front of me. His expensive cologne made my room smell nice and I wanted to take a deep breath.

"I didn't bring you here to keep you locked away. I enjoy your company Sam. You make me feel more like enjoying my life. I often overlook certain things that you remind me of in your excitement. Taking you with me is the main reason I brought you here to the city. First, I have to prepare you. You're not ready for this world yet."

He sounded like he had me here for more than a housekeeper. Men didn't take their housekeepers to parties and teach them to be more refined. Did they? I was pretty sure that even though I didn't know much about this life I did know that.

"But Hale, I'm your housekeeper," I told him.

He knelt down in front of me and gathered my left hand in both of his. "You're here to take care of things when I'm away. Yes, that's the truth. But surely you know that I brought you here for more than tending the penthouse."

He did? No, I didn't know that at all.

"Sam, you're a stunning woman. The first time I saw you I knew I would have to have you. I don't want for much but when I see something I want then I go after it. You're too talented and beautiful to be someone's housekeeper. You're meant for lights and parties. You're meant to shine. I intend to let that happen."

So he liked me. The funny feeling he gave me in my stomach when he flirted was mutual? "I'm trying to understand," I replied.

He stood and pulled me with him. Tugging me up against his body, his right hand slipped to my back, and I was firmly held flush with his chest. "Let me be more specific." He then lowered his head until his mouth brushed my neck, ear, cheek and lips. The small gasp of surprise that came from inside me was the opening he needed to have me. The warmth and taste of the wine filled my senses as he deepened the kiss and held me.

My knees began to go weak. I was torn between pleasure and shock. I wanted a kiss the night of the dance, but this wasn't the kiss I imagined. I'd seen kisses like this on the movies. It made you blush to watch it and here it was happening in actual life.

His hand then slid to my butt. He squeezed and I inhaled sharply, Hale continuing to taste me like his glass of rich wine, my head light and body tingling, anticipating what would happen next. This was enough to give a girl daydreams and make her silly for eternity.

When he cupped my face with his other hand his thumb brushed my cheekbone. It trailed down my neck until stopping just before he reached my breast. My nipple hardened in need and I couldn't believe I was reacting this way so quickly. There was an ache between my legs and I wanted to squeeze my thighs. I needed relief from what I was feeling and I was having trouble standing.

"That's why," he said softly as his lips finally broke. "We fit. Perfectly together."

I wanted more of that kissing and words weren't going to come to me right then. I stared wide-eyed and weak.

"I need to go now or we'll move this further than need be moved at the moment." He dropped his hands from my body and stepped back. "Enjoy your evening Sam."

Then the man was gone.

I inhaled deeply seven or eight times before sinking back down on my bed. The tingling was still there, still wanting relief. I was a virgin, but I wasn't ignorant. I knew what I needed to do.

When I heard the door close signaling he was gone I slid smoothly back on the bed. Slipped my hand down the front of my panties. The touch of my fingers against the swollen clit made me sigh with pleasure. I needed to finish what Hale had started.

With slow pressure I circled the sensitive nub and closed my eyes to reflect. Memories of his hands on my body, where I would've liked for him to touch, brought me to the release I required. I cried out, my legs shaking, as the wave of pleasure washed over my body to drown me.

This wasn't the first time I had done this. But it was the first time I had an actual face to accompany my imagination. The smell of his skin still clung to me. I ran my palms over my breasts, gently pinching my hardened nipples. He had called me beautiful, was attracted to me and he wanted me with him in the city. Sure he did things I didn't really like but he wasn't what I was used to. He was making concessions for me. I had to do the same for him. My body reacted to Hale. It enjoyed his touch and pressures. I wanted more. Had to have it. And to have it I would remain.

Twenty-Five

MY DREAMS WERE full of fairytales. Traveling the world, going to fancy parties, and even outrageous closets full of clothes. When I opened my eyes I felt ashamed of myself even though I couldn't exactly control my dreams. It still felt wrong to be so wrapped up in the things Hale could give me.

I liked him as a person. To me he was more than his money.

But would you like him if he lived in Moulton?

That was momma's voice in my head. Bringing me back to reality. The truth was, a part of me was superficial. I wasn't in love with Hale. I was fascinated with him because of the life he lived.

This was a part of my journey. It wasn't like I was marrying the man. I was working for him, and although he said he wanted more, and score one for momma because she'd just said that to me, I wasn't sure what more would be. Could I fall in love? Would it be easy because of all he could give me?

You were raised better than that. Momma's voice again. Ricocheting around in my head.

While trying to clear my thoughts I finished making up the

bed and dressing. Momma's voice finally left. Images of Hale did not. It was just after sunrise and although Felicity's note said Hale would awaken at eight ready for breakfast on the balcony with the morning paper, I wanted to have a head start making everything perfect. Plus, I really needed my own bite of breakfast and some coffee. I studied myself in the mirror. The new wardrobe that arrived last night had been surprising. Everything felt different. The fabric even smelled fancy.

Figuring out what I was supposed to wear everyday was confusing. The two really extravagant dresses hanging in my closet were the most mind boggling of all. Where would I wear those? Last night I'd slipped on the shoes that matched them and lapped the room a couple of times. They gave me the silly feeling of playing dress up. Like I was a child or something.

He'd even had panties and bras delivered. I wasn't sure why it mattered what I was wearing under my clothes. I figured no one saw that and my undies were just fine. But these felt nice. Satin and silk. Putting them on made me feel like a princess. After changing three times I decided that the black linen shorts and delicate looking sleeveless blouse were good enough for casual. Though they didn't feel casual in the least. The price tags were gone, but I had a feeling that clothing arriving without a price tag was too shocking for the average person to comprehend.

Cooking breakfast in this was going to make me nervous. He'd said not to unpack my bags, meaning he didn't want to see me in any of my own clothes. Hale wanted me dressed in what he had purchased and I would do what he said. I tried not to focus on the cost of my outfit. I pulled my hair back into a loose low braid and proceeded.

The penthouse was quiet. Just the light muffled sound of the busy city came through the windows. I went to the glass doors in the living room and stepped outside to take in the view. I needed reminding I was here. Everyday I would need reminding. I was afraid I would suddenly wake and this would all be a dream. I'd be back in Moulton at the bakery. Something I did not want. The part of my life that kept me in Moulton was over and done with forever. I hugged myself and smiled as I studied the city below me, bustling and colorful and pulsing, people hurrying about in their business attire, while others carried shopping bags. The tourists were obvious with their cameras and phones snapping photos for friends back home.

Soon I would be a part of that world. Hale would take me to parties and lunches. I would walk the streets in my expensive clothing just like I lived in a movie, one continuously playing for me. My smile grew as I imagined what life with Hale was going to be like in the future. Would he take me to his other homes? Would I travel with him on his plane? I had no idea what surprises were in store for Sammy Jo Knox from Moulton.

I wanted to see so much. Do and experience it all. New York City could never be uncovered, because there was so much inside it to reveal. And I wanted to peel it back. As much as I thought I could. That wasn't greed, now was it? Was my ambition blind to that? Was my desire to live my dream and its fancies arrogant self-absorption? These questions pinged in my head.

Turning around I went back inside and headed for the kitchen to cook. My stomach was rumbling loudly. I needed food to think about this. I knew if I called and asked momma, she would tell me "yes, you're being greedy." But then, of course, I could tell myself that momma didn't understand things. She saw them differently because of the way she had lived, which wasn't the life I desired. I was a dreamer. I chased after my dreams. I wanted so much more and I wouldn't feel bad about going after my goals. If I hadn't wanted more I would've missed this opportunity by being married to a guy in Moulton, when Hale stopped by the bakery. Things align and have a reason. That, I believe in my heart.

Knowing there was something bigger, a thing barely at the tips of my fingers, has kept me going since I was little. I loved the fantasies I created in my head. They were escapes from the reality I was born in, its hard edges and sharp nasty points, pricking my dreams everyday.

Now, here I was, living fantasies. I wanted to think that daddy was in heaven smiling down on what I was doing. He knew what I wanted to do. Not once had he told me I shouldn't.

I also wanted this life for my sisters. Even if they didn't for themselves. I knew if I could show them there were other options outside of Moulton, Alabama, they'd soon see things different. Momma was Moulton. I understood that. But I wanted to give her more. Less worries about money and the bakery. I would send cash home to make that happen, as soon as I got ahead.

Hale brought me here to change me. A part of me wanted that. To belong to the life he lived. But I was scared of what it all meant. This was going to be a huge leap. I had come and would somehow survive.

Twenty-Six

I HEARD HIS voice before I saw him. He was on his phone as he walked down the hallway from his room past the kitchen. I could tell from his tone it was business. He was annoyed and irritable and gesturing.

Moving quickly I finished up his breakfast. He wanted two poached eggs and kale salad, mixed with dried cranberries and walnuts. It didn't seem very filling to me. Nor did it look appealing. I was glad I wasn't expected to eat this. My sugary cereal with slices of banana would serve me well as usual.

"I can't move the meeting. I have a prior engagement. It's at seven and I won't miss it." As he walked back into the kitchen, Hale spoke into his slim, flat smartphone. I had his French pressed coffee prepared. The French press thingy had thankfully come with directions. I'd never seen anything like it. He took it from my hands sighing loudly.

"Lunch here will be the best I can manage. I'll be here at twelve like we planned. They can join me here. Otherwise this will have to wait."

Hale ended the call and slipped the phone into his pocket. He greeted me, but it took effort.

"Good morning Sam," he said with a tight smile. He didn't look as if the morning was good at all. If he'd let me fix him a real breakfast he might enjoy it better.

"I'll take my breakfast outside. Where is the paper?" He asked, walking quickly towards the exit of the kitchen.

I snatched up the paper I'd retrieved from the door and lifted his plate to follow. I wondered if this was what he wanted. Someone to wait on him hand and foot. I'd never been around a man who needed a servant. My daddy would've been slapped, if he'd asked my momma to serve him. But I was the hired help. Maybe this was a rich people thing. I had a lot to learn.

The romantic guy from yesterday was gone and in his place was . . . this. I wasn't here for romance anyway. At some point a line would be drawn. I guess Hale was drawing it now.

He took a seat at the table and I waited until he settled back in his chair. I then placed the plate to his front, positioning the paper to its left.

"Can I get you anything else?"

He looked at his food and then me. "This is perfect. Are you not eating?"

"I ate earlier this morning when I woke up."

He motioned to the seat across the way. "Please join me if you will. I hate to eat alone."

I liked it out here in the open with the energy of the city just below us. Maybe waiting and eating with Hale wouldn't be so bad. That is, if he wanted me here.

I took the seat across from his stare and he immediately studied my clothes. "Better. Much, much better."

Saying thank you seemed silly since he'd bought the clothing and knew what it looked like before. The fact that my clothes hadn't been good enough still bothered me, but this was different. I was wearing a work uniform. I guess that was how I'd look at it. I'd have to let that go. He might know what was best for me. Here anyway, in the city.

"I wasn't sure what to wear while working."

His smile was one of amusement. "You chose well. Did you try on the cocktail dresses?"

I assumed they were the fancy ones, so I hadn't done more than touch them. I was afraid of the price tags and fabric. "No," I replied, with a shake of my head.

"Make sure they fit and that you like them. You'll be needing them soon enough."

I would? He was ready to take me out in public? My heart rate increased and then I realized I might go into a panic if he did. Or if he kept talking about it.

"Will you be having a lunch meeting here?" I asked to change the subject. I would need to know how many were coming and what to prepare when they did.

He nodded. "Yes. For three."

Good. That would give me something to do until then. I hated feeling like my time was wasted.

"You can clean my bedroom and bathroom. I'm going to stay out here and handle a few calls. Hopefully I'll get a moment's peace, to read the paper without being bothered."

There was something else to do. I hadn't thought about that. I should get in a maid's frame of mind. He was confusing me with all this talk of parties and fancy clothes. I couldn't remember who I was.

"Okay," I said, instead of the "yes sir," which almost fell from my lips. I wasn't sure he'd like that very much. "Can I get you more coffee?" I asked.

He shook his head. "Not yet. Give me about fifteen minutes.

I'll be ready for another cup."

I glanced at my watch. He seemed to like things on a schedule. "I'll be inside cleaning if you need anything."

He tilted his head to look. Those eyes were something else. Straight from a magazine. He could easily model in his spare time. "Do you like it here?" he asked.

I nodded. "Yes. Yes I do."

A grin spread across his face. "Good. I like having you here." Then his hand reached forward to gently caress the inside of my wrist with his finger. "You make things that were dreary, exciting."

I wasn't sure how I was doing that exactly. But it made me smile and my cheeks heat up into a blush that he noticed in an instant. "I'm glad," I replied, almost breathless.

He chuckled and pulled his hand back. I hurried inside to take a deep breath and think about what he'd said. Hale was a confusing man. It didn't seem like he'd be anymore understandable today, tomorrow or forever. I wanted to please him, but a part of me worried about losing myself along the way. While I made his bed and put towels in his bathroom I thought about the luxury that surrounded him. This was a life he fit. I needed to taste it, but I wasn't really sure I'd ever belong like him. Like now, right now for instance, I wanted to put on cut off jeans, a tank top and knot my hair up. Pile it on top of my head. Although, that wouldn't do for here. I wasn't home working on the farm. I was where I'd always dreamed of being and I had to start trying harder to adjust and mold to this world. If I was choosing this life, then I would have to make it work, regardless of the changes involved. Hale had taken a chance by bringing me here and I'd also gambled by coming. Perhaps what would change would be me. A little, not a lot. I would take it a day at a time.

Twenty-Seven

"HE'S CHANGED YOUR clothing. I liked what you were wearing before." Ezra's voice made me jump and turn. He was standing in the kitchen's entrance. Without thinking I immediately responded. "I'm supposed to look a certain way. Ever heard of a uniform?" Even though it came out kind of harsh, Ezra's compliment made me feel good. He smirked, crossed his arms over his chest, then leaned against the doorframe. "I just hate to see him do it. There's nothing wrong with you now. But he'll change you, wait and see."

I turned back to the salad I was making. Him standing there like a cowboy in a painting made me a little nervous. There was no doubt the man was gorgeous. In that Texas cowboy way. Though I knew it was only an act, because he wasn't, he worked for Hale.

"Hale is outside with the other guest."

He didn't move. Although I wasn't looking at him I knew Hale hadn't budged. I had ears and the man was soundless. He replied, "I know where he is. I'm not in a hurry to join them."

Ezra was weird and strange. I didn't need him intruding with

Hale. I wasn't quite sure what there was between us, but this guy was an employee. He should care about upsetting Hale. Both of us had the same boss.

"Why're you in here with me when there's a meeting that doesn't include me? Shouldn't you be with them?" This time I turned to make him leave faster, though I figured he would do what he wanted.

"Not real big on Hale's meetings. I don't have to fuck with this one."

Oh, well, okay. I didn't know what to make of this man. Each episode with him became stranger. I wanted to dislike him, but there was something about him that was attractive, it drew you in. Maybe it was his personality. He didn't give a shit about much. Or seemed not to care. His vibe was more than dangerous, and that can be really sexy.

"I need to serve the appetizers." I lifted the tray of zucchini with the goat cheese tarts I'd made. It was a recipe Felicity had suggested that seemed easy enough. It gave me confidence for dishes that would take more time and contained various ingredients. I was thinking about this when Ezra moved towards me to take the tray from my hands.

"I'll take it when I go."

That didn't sound like a good idea. He was a guest of Hale's. A guest and an employee? This became more and more confusing.

"Uh, I better take it. That's my job."

Ezra studied me a little too closely. It made me feel like fidgeting and looking away, but I held his gaze and returned it.

"Are you scared of Hale?" When he asked me his voice dropped. It was lower and almost threatening. Frowning, I shook my head. "Why would I be scared of Hale?"

His entire body seemed to relax as he gave the tray back to me. "You take it then," he replied. Then he left without explanation.

I took a deep breath, tried to push it from my thoughts and focus on the job I was hired for.

I gave Ezra a minute to get outside before I followed with the tray I'd prepared. I thought about what momma would say, how she'd react to this: "Lord, that ain't enough to feed a man! Make a pot roast with potatoes and gravy!"

Smiling at the thought I took the food. Only Ezra seemed to notice me. I placed the appetizers on the table with his gaze against my skin. I glanced at Hale, who simply nodded, while speaking to the other guest. That was my dismissal.

Hurrying back inside I slid the glass. Ezra's focus was still on me. I was accustomed to the stares of men. I just wasn't used to the Ezra's. He might think this was some sort of game, but it was my future he was dealing with. I wasn't going to anger Hale, get fired and sent back to Moulton. Ignoring Ezra was best for the present. Even though he was making it hard.

The rest of the lunch was the same. Ezra watched me like a hawk. Hale acted as if I was invisible. I managed to behave in a way that I thought would make Hale happy.

When I heard them all leave I finished cleaning up the kitchen while waiting on Hale to come to me. He didn't say a word. I heard his footsteps down the hall and a door close behind him and then there was silence as usual.

I went outside to get the rest of the dishes and then made the kitchen perfect. After that I headed for my room. Hale was closed in his office and I could hear his voice through the walls asking questions. It was muffled, but I knew they were questions.

There was nothing for me to do. I wasn't sure I was allowed to go out. Was I to wait and expect to be needed? I laid down on the bed with a New Yorker magazine I'd found in the living room. I would read and see what happened. Or perhaps I would fall asleep. The sharp knock on my door sent me bolting upright in the bed like a child from a nightmare. I never took naps at home. This job and the city seemed to wear me to a frazzle. Everything was always in motion. Moulton, Alabama wasn't here. I hurried to the door to open it. Hale stood there with a grin on his face.

"Did I disturb your beauty sleep?"

"Sorry. I don't know what happened. I haven't done that very much. Not since I was a baby." I then blushed. "But, I don't remember. Being a baby that is." My God I'm babbling, babbling.

"You woke up early and spent the entire morning working and doing your job. It's okay to nap."

I was relieved to hear him say that.

"You are, however, wrinkled. Change into something else. We'll go out and explore."

I was wrinkled? Really? I glanced down and figured I still looked fine, but I didn't argue with the man. "Okay," I agreed. "I can't wait to see the city."

To be released from the penthouse I would do what he asked. I wasn't used to being indoors. It was beginning to feel like a jail and my boss was the jailer who kept me. Naw, that's too dramatic. I must be imagining things. Hale smiled and walked away.

I hurried to my closet, once again overwhelmed, with the selection I had to choose from. I managed to find a dress that looked classy but was casual enough for exploring. I chose a pair of sandals with a heel. I wasn't sure about walking all over New York, but there weren't any flats in the closet. I brushed my hair and put on some lip-gloss. Studied myself in the mirror. I was still Sammy Jo from Moulton. That hadn't changed a bit. But there was someone else in my reflection. There was polish and sophistication. I once dreamed that I would see myself dressed in clothes like these. But the reality was even more amazing. I was really living my dream.

Twenty-Eight

I THOUGHT WE would walk the streets. But again Hale surprised me. There was a black Mercedes waiting. When we stepped onto the curb Williams was there to greet us. He opened the door for Hale and myself to slide inside the car.

"Williams, it's so good to see you." The very first friend I'd made in the city was here to join our trip. He grinned and nodded his head.

"Get in the car Samantha." Hale spoke tightly from behind me. Breathing down my neck. I wanted to say more to Williams, but Hale seemed annoyed by my greeting, so I slid inside the car onto the smooth leather seats that were warm. Unlike the exterior, they were the color of butter and the temperature inside was perfect.

"Times Square," he ordered as Williams closed the door. His attention then turned to me. "You don't speak to the hired help as if they were your friends. They are my employees."

"But I'm the hired help."

His frown then eased to neutral. "Not exactly. You're not

like Williams. You're taking care of my place and I'm meeting your needs."

I bought the groceries, cooked and served his lunch and also the lunch of his associates. I cleaned the house and wore what he wanted. And was getting paid to do this. So yes, I was a hireling. An employee like Williams. But I also didn't want to argue because Hale was taking me out. I was no longer locked in the penthouse. Only seeing those he wanted me to see.

"Okay," I replied without interest. I wanted to say so much more, but I didn't, this life being foreign to me, and perhaps this behavior was normal. Being open to a different way was a must if I wanted to live here. Moulton wasn't the norm. Momma's program was nothing like this. Say, for example, if you tried to compare the sun to a forty-watt light bulb. Moulton being the bulb.

"What exactly do you want to see in Times Square? I've often wondered what attracts the tourist."

What you thought of when you heard the name of the city were Times Square and the Statue of Liberty.

"I've seen it on television since I was a kid. I want to stand in the middle and absorb it. Take it in like I own it or something."

Hale chuckled. "Fair enough."

I watched the city pass by from the window, wishing we were out there walking, soaking up the energy that rolled off the people as they hurried to their appointments. They had their coffee in hand, phones at their ears, with shopping bags or briefcases swinging. There was so much excitement that including myself seemed like the thing to be doing. I wanted to hustle somewhere.

"She's changing her shoes," I said in awe, as a woman came from the subway. She jerked off the sneakers she was wearing to slip on heels for the streets.

"That's the business class for you." Hale said it without emotion. I wasn't sure what he meant by that, but I thought it was incredibly cool.

A young guy started to walk into the street while staring down at his cellphone. I started to yell to stop him, when a yellow cab blared his horn. It flew right past him, barely missing his leg, the cab never slowing down. I then decided that phones in the streets were a major no-no for me.

"Do people get hit often?" I glanced at Hale who was also busy on his phone living the life of speed.

"Daily," he replied.

"That's seven dead people in a week. In Moulton that would take two years."

He stuck his phone in his pocket and finally looked up. "Let's go see Times Square. Then we'll go shopping on Fifth Avenue before we eat at one of my favorites. It's in the Meat Packing District. You'll like it."

That all sounded wonderful to me. "Okay," I agreed.

Before Williams stopped the car I could see it. The big, bright and shiny glowing place I'd daydreamed all my life. I was here. It was just like the movies. I wanted to push the car door open and leap from the vehicle running. I then thought about the cabbies and their obvious reluctance to slow for pedestrians in the street. I remained in the car with amazement. I didn't want to be killed while exploring.

"Is it all you thought it would be?"

"More," I replied honestly.

"Is this good sir?" Williams asked. He pulled up right beside what looked to be a massive M&M store.

"Yes. I'll text when we're ready." Hale told him with a passionless bluntness.

I started to say thank you to Williams, but bit my tongue instead. He got out of the car with my fingers on the latch, beginning to open my door. Hale put his hand on mine. "No. He gets the door."

Another thing I didn't understand. I was perfectly capable of opening my own. I didn't see why Williams had to. But I waited and let the man do it. The silliness piled and piled. As I climbed out I whispered a "thank you" before turning my attention to the screens, their colors running the square.

"Oh my. My, oh my."

I wasn't the only tourist here. They were everywhere. It was easy to see the majority of people in the square weren't New Yorkers. The busy suits and ties were absent. Just cameras, families, and what appeared to be a cowboy standing in his underwear. Oh, and also, there were cartoon characters and a sad looking Mickey Mouse.

"Why is that man in his underwear?" I asked Hale as he came up beside me. An Asian family was having its picture made with the almost naked man and his guitar. A line had formed behind them. There were females my age waiting with their phones, their sorority shirts identical.

"The Naked Cowboy," Hale responded. "One of the wonders of Times Square with its tourists." He didn't seem to think it was wondrous. His tone was again annoyed.

"He just poses for photos and whatnot? Or does he play the guitar and sing?"

Hale rolled his eyes. "He gets money for the photos. People tip him. Now, let's go stand in the middle and let you take it all in so we can go. There are more enjoyable parts of the city that don't include these people."

I was enjoying myself just fine right here, but I didn't say a word. I followed Hale to stand in the middle. I needed a picture of this. To print and send home to Hazel. She would squeal when she saw where I was.

"Will you take a photo of me?" I dug for my phone in the

chaos of my purse and the searching drew his attention.

"Of course," he replied. Then frowned at the sight of my purse. "After this we're buying you a new one. Several new purses in fact."

I glanced down at the purse my mother had made me. She'd sewn it for my graduation. I liked my purse. But it didn't match my clothing. There was an obvious difference and he saw it, another thing I wouldn't have imagined.

Handing him my phone I stood back and smiled. I extended my hands as if supporting the world, or more like Times Square in my palms. Very touristy indeed. Just as he took the photo a woman came up to his hip. She was painted metallic gold and wearing a tiny bikini. He frowned, "no thanks" was his sharp reply, though it didn't seem to faze her. She had money tucked in her bottoms. I assumed she was another of those photo people who get tipped for taking pictures. I was tempted to get one with her. Jamie would think it was hilarious.

"I've had all of this I can take. It feels and smells disgusting." Hale said it too loud and the gold woman left and then he came over to me. I agreed the smell wasn't very agreeable, but we were standing on the world's crossroads. Sometimes adventure was smelly.

"Let's go shop for the items you need."

He then pressed his hand on my lower back and led me to the waiting Williams. I didn't say a word.

Twenty-Nine

S HOPPING WAS MORE intense than I imagined. I picked some clothing but didn't get to wear it, because models wore it for me. I then chose the items I wanted and tried them on myself. When I thought we were done, because it took forever, we ended up somewhere else.

The last stop was Louis Vuitton. I bought two purses quickly. As quickly as Hale would allow me. They cost more than any automobile my momma ever owned. As exciting as it felt to have them, I felt guilty for taking them with me. I wasn't sure I wanted the life I was living, though I always thought I would. I guess adjusting could take some time. I'd dreamed of beautiful clothing, expensive meals and a life that was charmed. But the reality of it was different. Hale wasn't in love with me and I wasn't his Cinderella. There was nothing about him that was prince-like. I had no idea what I was to the man or what we were together. And it was I, Sammy Jo Knox, who was stuck in the middle of this "thing." Whatever this "thing" was becoming.

Several times throughout the day Hale would answer his

phone. I thought that might bring the shopping to an end. Deep down I wanted it to. The money he was spending increased my discomfort, because it wasn't necessary. If momma could see this she wouldn't approve. It was ego, extravagance and arrogance. Neither of the three did she care for. Was that why it bothered me so much? I knew momma wouldn't like it? She'd warn me and I would ignore it. What if this time she was right?

His phone rang again after Louis Vuitton and he checked it without responding. Looked at the screen and then held it. We were settled in the back of the car. I thought we might be going to dinner. Although, after the shopping, I wasn't sure he wanted to do that. He knew that the lavish treatment had set me off kilter a bit. Actually, it had floored me. He then turned to me and spoke.

"I need to go to dinner with a friend who is only in town tonight. You're not ready for that kind of thing." He then looked back at his phone. "Your clothing is, but the polish of the clothing isn't sufficient enough. I'll drop you off at the penthouse. You can put away your new things and enjoy the evening as you wish."

I wanted to sigh in relief. Being alone sounded good. I was always tense with Hale. Unsure what he'd say or do next. I didn't want to feel this way. If I could just put my finger on what had changed that was making me nervous around him.

When Williams parked at the penthouse I was anxious to escape the car. To return to the jail I'd wanted to flee earlier in the day. I was tense from my time with Hale. I wasn't typically like this.

He stepped onto the curb then held out his hand for me to be helped from the car. I could do it myself, but I let him. It seemed rude not to do so. Once outside he pressed a kiss to my cheek and spoke softly into my face.

"Williams will deliver your things after he's dropped me off. I'll see you in the morning Samantha."

Then he climbed back into the car. Williams closed the door

behind him and hurried back around to leave. I didn't watch them go. I was ready to get back inside.

"Man, I need a break."

I'd looked forward to going into the city. Hale had made it something else. The shopping had been stressful and confusing. Why did I need so much? I liked my comfortable clothing and wanted to be able to wear it, especially when touring the city. What I'd imagined I would do was walk the streets and eat the food vendors were selling. Not be whisked from place to place. The way Hale was showing me the city wasn't my idea of an adventure.

He'd be leaving soon though. Hale said he didn't stay but a few days a month so my solo time was coming. I could do exactly as I'd dreamed. When I stepped from the elevator to head for the penthouse my eyes landed on Ezra. I froze. Couldn't move. He was dressed as casually as he'd been this morning. Relaxed, he leaned on the wall. Whatever it was he did, didn't require business attire. I couldn't imagine Ezra being bossed. Taking orders didn't seem like his style. There was a dangerous air about him. Yet, he didn't scare me a bit.

"Hale won't be home until late." I then forced myself forward to the door. I wasn't going to stare at the man. He'd think I'd lost my marbles. Although, he was nice to stare at.

"Yes, I know. I came to take you to dinner."

What? That got my attention. I paused and looked up at him. "Hale wouldn't like that at all."

Ezra smirked as if that were funny. "It would seem you're figuring him out."

He was amused, but I was not. I then entered the code to the penthouse and stepped inside the door.

"If there isn't anything I can do for you, then I will see you some other time."

Ezra didn't respond. Instead he followed me inside and stopped, inches away from my body. His warmth made me tremble and shiver. I forced my eyes to lift. They met his, waiting on mine.

"We can have dinner here. I'll be glad to cook."

Again, this was not okay. What was Ezra up to?

"I don't think that would be appropriate."

Ezra shrugged. "I'm not worried about appropriate. Sammy Jo, please relax." He then walked past me towards the bar making himself at home. I watched him pour himself a whisky over three ice cubes before he turned back to me. "Care for a drink?"

I shook my head no and huffed.

He took a sip and the way his throat muscles flexed were as appealing as everything else. I jerked my gaze off him and stared at the windows wondering if I should call Hale. I didn't want to get Ezra in trouble, but then I wasn't sure he cared. He didn't exactly seem the type to cower to a wealthy man. It was almost as if he mocked Hale.

"I'm not leaving Sammy Jo. Hale isn't coming back tonight. I know where he is and the person he's with. I'm here to keep you company. Nothing more than that."

He was here to keep me company? So Hale knew he was here? Why hadn't Hale just told me?

"Why? I don't need any company." I wasn't sure what I was saying.

He didn't respond right away. Ezra walked over to the balcony doors. I waited in silence for his answer.

"Because I like being around you. You're different from the rest of this city. More of what I knew, what I miss. You bring back the forgotten I suppose. It's pleasant."

That astounded and intrigued me. "You mean your home? Your town in Texas?" I thought Alabama must be similar to Texas.

Not that I'd been to Texas. Maybe little towns were alike.

"Something like that," he responded. "Sometimes missing is missing. Doesn't matter where the place might be."

Thirty

"WHAT IS IT you do for Hale exactly?" I wanted to understand their arrangement. How it started. Where it would go.

Ezra took another drink. Grinned and held it for a second. I wasn't sure why that question was funny. I also didn't want to enjoy the way he appeared when amused. Which, I was currently doing, while staring at the man like an animal.

"It's complicated Sammy Jo. I don't work for Hale, not exactly. Not the way you think."

"Are you partners?" I thought that would make more sense. Maybe allow him to define it. They looked like they stepped from two different worlds. The same went for Hale and myself.

He laughed, said "no," then laughed even louder. That was oddly attractive. I had to stop thinking of Ezra as attractive. That was not okay.

I could see I wasn't going to get any information so I gave up on that topic. I decided to then become bitchy. Might as well see what would happen: "my clothes will arrive soon enough. I need to put them away. Your company is a hindrance to me." Did I just use the word "hindrance?" What the hell was wrong with me?

Ezra continued his study of my face, that look of his intriguing. "Maybe I do," he replied.

Maybe he what? Needed the company? Sighing, I dropped my purse on the table that led into the kitchen. "Fine then, do what you'd like. I'm going to get some water."

I didn't look back at Ezra, hoping he wouldn't follow. The man was downright confounding. He confused my brain to no end. Of course, my body was attracted. I'd be lying if I didn't admit that. But Ezra was hiding something. I could see it in the depths of his eyes. He was watching to see if I could figure the reason they needed one another to thrive.

I knew Hale wouldn't want him here. At least I didn't think he would. Was that why I'd asked him to leave? Or was it the mystery around this man Ezra that bothered and forced me to push him? I glanced back at the door when I was safely in the kitchen, thinking about momma's reaction. She wouldn't approve of this man. He wasn't polished, so he wouldn't scare her. She liked the good ole boys. Although, Ezra wasn't one of those, he just had their appearance and style. I wondered if he was even from Texas.

After fixing my water I took a slow drink and walked back into the foyer. I knew he hadn't left. He would tell me if he was leaving. At least I thought he would. He wasn't in the living room, but I could see him outside on the balcony. Going to my room seemed rude. Even though it was probably smart. Though I admit, I wasn't really smart around Ezra. He was entirely too seductive.

The sound of the city hit my ears as I stepped outside to confront him. Ezra glanced back at me. "I was debating if you'd hide in your room or come and visit with me."

So much for my confrontation. "I thought about it, then I didn't."

"Don't doubt it. You strike me as sharp. Which is why you're working for Hale." When he didn't finish I finally spoke up to relieve our momentary silence. "Finish that comment please." I demanded, rather than asked. He didn't seem to mind my aggressiveness, his gaze now back on the city.

"You're not Hale's typical choice. You don't fit the mold."

"His choice in maids?"

Ezra turned to me. "You know what I mean Sammy Jo. You're smart. Don't be naïve."

I wanted to throw my water in his face. It was the way he said "naïve." But I didn't, because Ezra was right. I sounded backwards, dumb and naïve. I knew exactly what Hale had planned. He'd told me as much when he hired me.

"There's a mold?" I needed clarification. I knew his last housekeeper was old and feeble and had retired when the job was too strenuous. It wasn't like he hired girls that often, to eventually . . . what? To date?

"Typically the women he hires, for starters, aren't very likable. They're digging for gold and are here for a reason, to become the wife he doesn't have. One he doesn't need. He's built for marriage about like me and I tell you I don't want that."

Ezra had spoken in the plural. Said the words "the women he hires." Was I simply the next in a line? Hale made it sound like he needed me here. Like he'd found me and wanted me near him. Surely he didn't hire girls, clothe them and plan these events, as part of a wife finding process. He wasn't like that. I knew it.

"I'm not exactly sure what you mean."

Ezra finished off his whiskey. "Then maybe you are naïve."

Not the answer I was looking for. I fought the urge to stomp my foot and demand he answer my question. I deserved an explanation.

"Who do you think worked here before you?"

"An older lady that retired. She'd been working for Hale forever."

Ezra looked disgusted. "That's what he told you?"

I nodded.

"Fuck," he muttered.

I hoped he'd elaborate. I realized from his reaction that I wasn't told the truth, but then, who to believe? Hale or Ezra? Which? I didn't know. Ezra was a stranger to me. He could be causing trouble. Hale had brought me here, given me this life, while Ezra was a guy who'd annoyed me from the very first minute I met him.

"Maybe you need to go." I was feeling more and more confident, without really understanding why. I didn't want to be angry any more.

"I'll go. But you're going to need me. Eventually. Trust me on that."

He'd said something similar before. His certainty began to worry me. It wasn't like he was trying to convince me. He was warning me. That was it. He made it exceptionally hard to ignore.

"Okay," I said. "I hear you." I didn't say anything else. I had nothing more to say. I wasn't sure I believed this man. It seemed unfair to trust him over Hale.

Ezra started to walk back inside. Just as he reached the glass, he stopped and turned back to me. I realized I was holding my breath, afraid of what he would say. I wanted to be alone with my thoughts.

"Be careful. Pay attention. Don't assume that anything is a gift."

He then went through the entry and closed it behind him without waiting for my rebuttal, any question I might have had. I didn't follow Ezra. I stood there replaying his words in my head, again and again, over and over, like a recorder was lodged in my brain. I was careful and did pay attention. It was his comment on the gifts that bothered me. I wasn't comfortable with what Hale had bought. If Ezra was being honest, if there'd been a string of women, then what, what would I do? Do I stay here or go back to Moulton? This remained an opportunity. A chance I'd never had.

That evening my mind ran through its scenarios until I couldn't imagine another. Some were terrifying, while others made good sense. By the time I closed my eyes, I was sure I was overreacting. Time with Hale would ease my mind.

Thirty-One

WHEN MY EYES opened it was dark outside. I rarely woke up in the middle of the night, even when my sisters kneed me. I was a heavy sleeper. Frowning, I rose to check the time, the bedside clock dimly glowing. It was a little after two in the morning. I considered going back to sleep, but wanted to check the apartment. Something must've awakened me. A sound, maybe some street noise?

Slipping out of the satiny sheets I walked to the bedroom door. Opening it slowly, things seemed quiet and then I heard the feminine giggle, followed by Hale's deep voice. It was coming from his bedroom. There was a bump, then another laugh. I stood there wondering if this was real or was I asleep and dreaming. Would Hale bring a woman into the penthouse where I was sleeping to have . . . what? What was I thinking? To screw while I was present? To have sex right down the hall?

There was a moan and the woman cried "Hale!" which was met by a muffled "take it!" I froze with my head craned staring at his door, awake and aware and angry. This was awkward and confusing. Especially after what Ezra had shared and the way Hale had kissed me.

I listened as the moans grew louder, her cries increasing and when I couldn't stand it I reentered my room, sliding my feet, the door blocking the noise. It must've been their walk down the hallway that opened my eyes to begin with.

Sleep wasn't going to come now. My mind was too busy spinning. Was she the friend in town for the night he had to so urgently meet with? Why hadn't he said "I have a date," and then it would've been clear. But he chose to overwhelm and groom me with the shopping, which I thought meant something else. His signals made no sense. He did whatever he wanted.

Ezra was right about one thing. If I pretended it was something else, I was being naïve and stupid. He'd spent thousands of dollars on my wardrobe and purses, but exactly for what and why? To have the proper appearance when we dated? Was that really what I'd be doing? My job in New York City?

A loud female cry made it through the walls, followed by an extended groan. Great, they were getting louder. Just what I wanted to hear. I covered my ears with the extra pillow and closed my eyes till they finished. Hopefully, it wouldn't last long. Tomorrow I would address this with Hale. He needed to return the clothing or at least take back the purses. He didn't need me to go to parties. I was here to work for him. If he was planning on having sex with others, in his room so I could hear it, then this wasn't a relationship. We weren't headed in a romantic direction. Even the wealthy and the privileged had to have scruples and morals.

It wasn't until the penthouse quieted that I finally fell back to sleep. It was a fitful sleep with dreams of Moulton, Hale, and oddly Ezra.

I stood in the kitchen wondering what to do about breakfast

for the two. I hadn't heard Hale's guest leave. I supposed she'd be eating as well. There were no directions from Felicity on how to handle overnight guests. It was left to me to figure this out and to be really uncomfortable while doing it.

My best assumption would be to prepare enough for both when they awakened. If she didn't stay I'd put the extra away and eat it later myself. That sounded better than pretending like I didn't know she was here. I began washing and slicing the fruit.

Once his guest left we were going to discuss this. I wasn't sure what I was going to say but we had to talk this through. To come to some agreement. I didn't intend to "date" him if he was going to bring other women up to the penthouse to screw. That was mean and rude.

I prepared a fresh fruit tray then began making the crepes. Felicity left me a recipe. It wasn't until I had the turkey bacon cooked that I heard the footsteps behind me. Turning, I saw her there. She was tall and blonde and the towel she was wrapped in barely covered her body. Her exposed skin was tan. She was a model, obviously a model. A gigantic, perfect woman. I wanted to stab her with my fork.

"I thought I smelled food," she said, with a delicate childish yawn. "Could you bring it to the bedroom in fifteen minutes? I need to wake Hale up first."

I would be delivering breakfast in bed. Awesome. What a fun morning.

"Sure," I responded to the woman. I could've caved in her head with that vase.

Without another word she turned to leave, then paused to spin on her runway. "I don't drink coffee either. I'll need green tea without sweetener. Not too warm. Do you hear me?"

Before I could respond she was gone.

I knew there was an extensive selection of teas in the walk in pantry. I'd seen them there arranged. Apparently she also knew he'd have what she wanted to drink.

I started for the pantry when his bedroom door opened for heavier footsteps, headed in my direction. "I have appointments India. I told you last night." Hale's voice sounded annoyed.

"So you're going to fuck me for hours, then send me packing like a whore?"

"You stayed the night. Jesus, what more did you want?"

"Oh, I don't know, maybe breakfast!"

"I fed you dinner. Now please leave. I have work to do and this is wasting my time. Dress and get the hell out."

I heard her heels click on the marble as she muttered "you fucking bastard." I wasn't arguing with her on that one. He was being terrible.

"Last night you sure made it sound like you wanted more of me!"

"Last night is over. Time for you to leave," Hale responded cold and unemotional.

I didn't look for the tea. I left the pantry and went to make the French pressed coffee Hale drank every morning. This was even more uncomfortable than last night's marathon sex. Only this time I couldn't hide in my room with a pillow over my head.

"Never again you shit. I'd heard you were a dick, but I didn't believe it, so I thought I would give you a chance."

"I'd heard you were fucking crazy and should've listened to the fellow that told me."

She spouted off a string of curse words then the door slammed behind her. I jumped, hoping she was gone, although I'd soon face Hale and the mood he was in made me nervous and frightened. All the discussing I'd planned didn't seem like a good idea.

"I'll be outside. Bring my breakfast. I already have the paper."
When Hale said it, it gave me a start. I glanced over my shoulder to see him leaving, our talk now postponed. I didn't have the nerve to confront him. Not with him like this.

Thirty-Two

*H*E DIDN'T SPEAK or look up from his paper. It went a long way to achieving his goal of pissing me off again. I'd gotten nervous listening to Hale abuse India and now I was disgusted with his behavior.

When he finally left for his meeting he said "I'm leaving" and then closed the door. That was it. No explanation. No apology for the sex-fest I'd heard. It was as if I wasn't even there.

I tried to fill my time cleaning the place without allowing my thoughts to drift in the direction of what he'd done. In that, I admit, I failed. I yanked off his sheets like I was tearing out hair, calling him a bastard while I made it.

Once that was done I decided to get dressed in the clothes I'd brought with me. It was time to see the city, minus Hale bearing down on me, wanting to control my movements. There wasn't any reason for me to wait on a call or an order from him in person. I had the phone and would keep it on me. Rifling through my bag I found my blue jean shorts, a tank top and my boots. I took a moment to pull my hair up, then I grabbed momma's purse. I was dressed for the streets of Moulton, Alabama and not the busiest city on earth. Oh well, I was comfortable. It was New York City on my terms. I didn't care at the moment if he knew or not and I did not need his permission. At least he never said I did.

Glowing with pride I stepped through the door before my mission was suddenly stopped. Ezra slid from the elevator. Why was he back? Again!

"Good, you're dressed. I was coming to get you. Does lunch sound good? It's on me."

What?

"Hale won't be home until tonight. He's kinda, somewhat busy." Ezra added this when I didn't move or speak, because I guess he felt he had to.

"I'm not hungry. I was going to roam." Spending the day with Ezra wasn't what I'd planned. He reported to Hale whatever we did and I'm sure the things I said. Really, I had no earthly idea what he did or why he was here.

"Then we can roam together. You'll eventually get hungry and the street vendors here are my personal friends by name. I know the best by the color of their carts. Remember Sammy Jo, I'm from a small town, and our backgrounds are pretty similar. Working parents, low income, etc. I'm basic, just like you. Had dreams and I achieved them. The face of success isn't always wealth. You can be yourself and keep your soul, because the world has places for that. It isn't always mean and suspicious. Looking to kill and eat you."

I wanted to eat without the speech. And if he knew the best it would be like a movie, where the characters ate in the streets. It sounded silly, but I dreamed about that.

"It'll be boring Ezra. You know it like the back of your hand. I need to find it for myself." I argued, though I actually wanted, a map to where the vendors were.

"Please, let me decide that. If I get bored I'll recommend where to go and leave you as you wish."

That wasn't a bad idea. "I'm walking," I said, "not going in a car like Hale made me do."

"Good," was his reply. "The city is seen from the end of the nose and with every step we'll take."

Profound, and I was stuck. There was no getting out of this. I liked Ezra more and more. He had a way about him that was hard to ignore. He was a playful little boy under all that toughness. Determined, but really fun.

"Okay," I agreed, tugged my purse on my shoulder and headed to the elevator. He held the door open for me.

"I like your clothes," he said as they closed.

I felt his gaze and it made my skin warm. Tingly, but not like the cold. It was as if I were a view that Ezra was taking in. Hale had never done me like that. It was always me who took him in, while he seemed to remain aloof, like some other thing needed doing. They were wildly different men.

"What do you do for Hale?" I asked, turning to meet his stare, which was still fixed on my body. Hale's world wasn't here anymore. Not until I brought it back in.

"I don't actually work for Hale." His eyes left my frame. Returned to the elevator doors.

"That's not an answer Ezra." I said it matter of fact, without realizing I'd barked it.

"No, I guess it isn't." After he agreed the doors split open and he said "after you."

"So if he finds out we spent the afternoon together he won't fire you or even get angry?"

Ezra chuckled. "No."

He didn't give me a definite answer, but the warmth of the breeze met my face. The sound of the city was there. I decided

I'd let it go. I would enjoy what I had, including Ezra's company, so I changed my attitude.

"Which way?" I glanced from left to right.

"Um, Ezra, I don't know." I honestly had no idea. "Which way is the best food vendor?" I hoped he didn't hear my stomach growl.

He pointed left. "Thought you weren't hungry?"

I shrugged. "Might've lied."

Ezra appeared amused. Hale would've been angry or annoyed. Their differences were stacking up daily. And why was I even measuring these men against each other in the first place? After what Hale did last night any chance for us was gone. I would work for him. That was all.

Then, of course, whatever their agreement, Ezra might be unavailable. What I needed were friends outside their world. A life when I wasn't working. I was ready for Hale to leave. His monthly visit had been long enough.

"What've you seen of the city so far?"

"Hale took me to Times Square and then we went shopping." That, I didn't want to repeat.

"Then let's go get you the best tamales you've ever had in your mouth. Then I'll show you a slice of the city."

I'd never had tamales. It sounded really exciting. Better than the hotdog I'd envisioned.

"Sounds like the perfect plan. What places are you going to show me?"

Finally, I was getting to see it. And with someone who knew it on foot.

"Well, you're a newbie, so I figured we'd begin with a ferry ride on the boat to Ellis Island. Go and see the Statue of Liberty. Might take up our entire afternoon, but we can always do this again. New York can take a year to cover the museums and the haunts of the tourists and the locals. Then you'd still lack hundreds."

I wanted to clap with glee like a five year old with ice cream. That was exactly what I wanted to do. Hugging Ezra seemed a tad too aggressive, but I almost did it anyway.

"Thank you," I said instead. Settling for a more acceptable means to demonstrate my bubbling joy.

"Don't thank me yet Sammy Jo. Getting on the ferry is a pain in the ass, but it's worth it in the long run."

I had no doubt that it was.

Thirty-Three

*H*E WAS WRONG. Everything was perfect. Nothing was a pain in the ass. I soon realized I could act really silly and Ezra thought it was hilarious. Seeing the things I'd only read about made the little girl inside me giggle. I couldn't take enough photos, read enough monuments or ask more stupid questions. Ezra patiently answered them all. For the sake of my sisters I was like a tourist guide who could spout any detail desired. I did not miss a thing.

By the time we got back to the penthouse it was after six and I was nervous. Hale hadn't called me all day. I was worried that my being gone like this was going to make him angry. He'd never been angry with me before, but I'd now seen his ugly side and I didn't want to turn it on me.

"Hale may be back," I said. We were walking toward the entrance. I should've been thanking Ezra for the day or a host of things. But my focus was on Hale coming back. My perfect day was about to be marred by Hale shutting it down.

"He isn't."

He was sure but didn't elaborate.

"There's the best Chinese food in the states nearby. I can call and get us some dinner. Trust me, you won't regret it."

So Ezra wasn't leaving? If he was right and Hale wasn't coming back then we did need to eat somewhere. I enjoyed being around him. He wasn't concerned about Hale, so maybe I shouldn't be either. He knew him better than me.

"Okay," I agreed. "Sounds great." He'd given me his entire day. If he wanted to eat dinner with me, then I should be accepting, not nervous. He seemed to know where Hale would be.

Stepping into the penthouse I was shaky. Not sure how to handle Hale. He might send me packing back to Moulton. But Ezra was right. Hale was gone. The place appeared the same as I had left it. "You're right. He's not here." I then sat my purse down on the table and wondered if I should go change it. Once again, I feared his wrath and I didn't like that feeling. But you were supposed to want to please your boss. That was the normal procedure. Correct?

"He won't be back until much, much later," Ezra replied without concern. How he knew this was true I couldn't be sure, but he seemed to be secure in the knowing. I forced myself to relax and trust him.

"Would you like something to drink? He's got everything you could want."

"I'll get it. What about you? A glass of wine?"

I hadn't drunk alcohol since arriving here. I was still under age, though that wasn't the reason, I didn't feel comfortable drinking around Hale and I had no explanation for that.

"I'll go get a glass of water."

I didn't wait for him to ask me why or insist I drink the wine.

"Okey dokey," he casually responded.

Stepping into the kitchen it gave me time to think about what was happening. I'd enjoyed my time with Ezra. There was a touch of something there. Anxiousness, or maybe excitement, neither one an acceptable feeling. He either worked with Hale or in Hale's vicinity, though I couldn't figure that out. He was nothing like Hale, but oddly enough, what I thought Hale would be like, the very first time I met him. Today, for instance, he'd liked making me smile, telling me jokes and when I wanted to do something he didn't frown or suggest something else. We went to it and did it that second.

I got my water and walked back into the living room. Ezra was standing by the windows with a glass of whiskey in his hand. "The wine Hale keeps is excellent. You should try a glass and relax. You're so pent up, nervous and scared. I wouldn't stay if I thought it would cause you problems. Trust me on that Sammy Jo."

He came directly to the point and I liked that.

"Okay," I heard myself say.

Ezra smiled and the grin made my heart do a stutter like it was trying to tell me something. He was really nice to look at. Now that I didn't dislike him so much, I could admit the man was beautiful.

"Good!" was his jovial reply. He walked back to the bar and opened a bottle, pouring wine in a massive glass. The liquid was so red it was black.

"I'm not a big drinker," I admitted.

Ezra smirked this time. "I didn't exactly peg you as a whorish party animal. The glass is big so you can move it around. Look at it. Shit like that. I've never really understood it myself. I'm not exactly a connoisseur."

He was teasing me and self-deprecating, all at the very same time. That was really hard to do, to make fun of yourself and another without being mean about it. Taking the glass I couldn't help but smile up into his face and teeth. He made being away from everything that I loved easier, which gave me peace.

Taking a small sip the liquid was rich and expensive tasting on my tongue. You could actually smell the dollars rising from the glass. The only other wine I had sampled was some homemade swill in Moulton. Ben's dad had made a batch from blackberries with a tart, sour taste. It didn't have the smoothness of what I was drinking. This was velvet on your tongue.

"I don't know much about wine, but this sure tastes nice goin' down."

"It should," he replied with a laugh. "It's four hundred dollars a bottle." He then nodded his head out to the balcony as I collected myself from the floor. "I've already called in our order. They'll ring me when they arrive downstairs. Let's go outside and enjoy the evening."

Although this wasn't a date or anything romantic I felt like it was becoming that. We'd done things I once imagined I'd do with Hale, but now I didn't want to be around him.

"When do you leave?" I asked him, once we stepped outside. That suddenly made me sad. The idea of Ezra's going. I hadn't been alone today. I liked having him around.

He shrugged. "Never know. When the job calls I move quick and immediate."

And what job was that exactly?

"Are you ever going to tell me what it is you do?"

He didn't look directly at me but I could see his shoulders tense.

"No," was all he said.

He had his reasons for being quiet. And just because he'd shown me a good time didn't mean his secrets were mine. I wanted to know more about Ezra. My curiosity was subject to fancy. My imagination got the best of me.

"I worked at a bakery with my mom, until Hale came in one day." I told him because I wanted to share my life. The connection was important to me.

"Do you miss it?" His stare came back and was riveted.

"I miss my family and friends, not Moulton. Coming here was a much better choice."

"And is this world what you thought it would be?"

I thought about that question. Was it? Yes and no. "Not completely. But I've only just begun."

He appeared thoughtful and reserved. "New York City isn't your final destination?"

I shook my head. "No it's not. It's the beginning of a very long trip."

"Don't let your desire to see it all make you loose sight of what's best."

What exactly did he mean by that?

"What exactly do you mean by that?"

He turned his baby blue gaze to the city. "Don't simply settle for what you think can fulfill the dream you have. Some roads to a dream, or through it, can actually be paths to a nightmare."

Again he was warning me. But why and from what? Did he worry about me with Hale?

"I don't want more from Hale than a job." I blurted it like a confession.

"Yes, but Hale wants you. He'll want more and more each day."

I finished my wine, let the warmth relax my body and then Ezra filled it again. I drank my second glass while I watched him get the order from the takeout guy in the hallway. He then grabbed a couple of plates. He was comfortable here as if he knew the place well. Ezra did more than I realized.

The mystery around him seemed less important after my second glass. When he filled it again the mystery of wine was the best idea to muse on. I'd have to investigate it further.

Thirty-Four

EZRA HAD BEEN correct. The Chinese food was delicious. The best I'd ever eaten. Being this close to that particular restaurant was a major perk for me. I'd be ordering again for sure.

He spent the meal telling stories from his past. I laughed for an hour and a half. They weren't detailed nor did they give me any insight into what he actually did. But they showed me who he was as a person. He wasn't from wealth like Hale. That much I'd gotten from the tales. I also didn't think he respected Hale. Or if he did he didn't show it.

The buzz from the wine relaxed me and I enjoyed my dinner immensely. Just as much as Ezra's company. When he laughed his eyes lit up. There was a beauty in the flash that I wanted to admit before I blurted it out. I didn't think he was starving for complements, or sponging attention from others, but he was, and he was pretty. Although I didn't want him to think I was flirting. I didn't know what to do.

"Another glass?" he asked, standing up from the table.

I shook my head no. I was tipsy. Strike that, I was drunk. "No thank you. I've had my fill."

He nodded and glanced at the time on his phone. "I need to be going. I'll clean this up first."

I quickly stood to help him. "You can go ahead and go. I've got this. Really I do."

He paused and his eyes locked mine. "You're not my fucking house cleaner sweetheart. This was my idea. My job." His smile was the size of a planet. I began hyperventilating. I wasn't going to argue with him. "At least let me help a touch. I need to contribute something."

"You've contributed yourself. I enjoyed the day and the evening more than anything I've done in years. This has been peace for me."

My cheeks flushed and I wanted to tell Mr. Ezra about his magical smile, how he made me feel, but I feared the wine was talking and my clothes may land on the floor. That didn't seem like the end of the world. The idea was growing on me. I picked up my plate and an empty box then followed him inside the apartment.

"Hale will be home within the next thirty minutes. As much as I like your clothes I think you'd better change into that ridiculous shit he bought for you to wear."

I'd wondered about that earlier. But hearing Ezra say it like he was protecting me made me more alert and wary. Was he afraid Hale would get angry and send me back to Moulton? Or was there more to his suggestion?

"Does Hale have a temper?" I asked.

He paused and held the garbage in his fist. With a sigh he turned back to me. "Hale is an intense man. He likes things to be in his favor. You work for the man so you follow his rules. Even if he has other plans, that eventually, do include you. Just be careful and" he extended his hand "give me your phone so I can put my number in it. That way if you need me for anything, and I mean anything at all, you call and I will answer."

I gave him my phone and watched as he saved his number into it. Somehow, I felt safer. And I didn't think that was wine.

"Have I made a mistake coming here?"

He didn't respond at first. After a moment he shook his head. "No. You'll be fine."

I wanted to ask more questions while the wine was making me brave. But I didn't, because they'd go unanswered.

"Thank you for your time," I said.

Ezra put his plate in the dishwasher. Reached for mine and did the same. When he was finished he closed on my body. I thought he was going to make another comment but his hand slid into my hair and tilted my head to the side. I was so immersed in the look from his eyes that when his lips touched mine I was startled. The soft warmth of his mouth sent a jolt of electricity through everything that was inside me. I grabbed his arms and held on tight. He deepened the kiss as his tongue touched mine and I shivered from the pleasure of it all. The richness of the whisky on his breath fit his mouth like his shirt fit his body. It was exactly how I thought he would taste. Like something dark, but thoroughly exciting.

I was leaning into Ezra when he finally pulled back, his blue eyes sinking their depth. "I need to go. Better go now." His voice was a husky whisper.

I started to say something but he turned and left, quietly exiting the apartment. Standing there alone I suddenly felt cold. I touched my lips and the warmth from his lingering kiss remained and I could still taste him. My heart was thumping rapidly in the center of my chest and I wanted to run after Ezra. That was silly and caused by the wine. As pointless as my attraction to the man. Then again, he'd shown me what I always desired, but was yet to experience in this life. I hoped Hale would be like him, but he wasn't and that wouldn't change.

And now he was out of my reach. Ezra would soon be gone. I didn't know where or even why he was leaving and his job seemed to be a secret. All he could do was what we'd done today, which was fleeting and had become a memory.

The pleasure I'd experienced turned to an ache at the thought of not having it again. I'd been selfish with expectation. When it was gone it was just as quick, as having dreamt about perfection in the first place. For the very first time I understood longing. If that solitary kiss had made me feel alive then what more would happen when he loved me. If he could ever love me at all. Could ever want a girl like me. Sammy Jo Knox from Moulton. And I didn't even know his last name.

There was a sound at the door and my head jerked around to see if Ezra was waiting. To say something more, or anything less, or just to stand and permit my staring. Hale then stepped inside and my hopes became pure anxiety. His gaze took in my clothing and the look of displeasure on his face was rude and obvious. "I didn't buy you decent clothing for you to wear that stuff around. What if I'd had company? Is this how I'd want you to look?"

I was being scolded like a child.

"No," I replied. "No it wouldn't."

"I don't want to come home to find you dressed like this. Never again Samantha."

Again he called me Samantha. A name that wasn't mine. Just like the clothes I was wearing.

"Go change if you intend to stay awake and visit with me this evening."

I turned and headed to my room. Not because I wanted to visit with Hale, but because I knew if I didn't change soon his anger would linger until he would leave and then return when he came back. Soon I'd be alone and this phase would be finished, at the least for a couple of weeks. I could tolerate as much as Hale could deliver and I imagined that was a lot but a load I was willing to bear.

Thirty-Five

*T*HE LAST THING Hale had said last night was "I'll be back in fourteen days. We will then be attending a party and I expect you to behave like a lady. Not an inbred girl from the sticks." And I said nothing in return. As if I deserved the command. I was to spend my time getting online and researching how to properly act. To work on my speech and pay attention to the way I pronounced my every word. It was a humiliating conversation.

When the door closed behind him I was relieved he'd only kissed my cheek. I wasn't in the mood to be touched by the man after being informed a complete overhaul was how I would stay in New York. I knew I didn't fit into Hale's glitzy world, but I didn't take this job and move to the city thinking someone would rubber stamp me and turn me into a talking robot. And what purpose did his control really serve? There was no affection between us. We didn't have a chance at a future.

After a day with Ezra I knew what I wanted. Hale would re-main my boss. But we'd never be anything more. Surely he could see that too. If he wasn't concerned with attraction or connection between the people we ultimately were, maybe it was personal appearance? I didn't know him at all.

For the moment I was glad he was gone. I had too much on my mind and the cleaning of the penthouse wasn't enough to encourage me. Calling home wouldn't be a good idea. Momma would recognize the frustration in my voice. She'd know something was wrong and question me until I admitted it. Going home to Moulton in the future kept me twisted in tangled knots. Staying here would only be possible if Hale kept me as an employee. I no longer wished to attend those parties and classy events I'd longed for. Hale was heartless and the way he treated other people was a thing I would never accept.

The next two days I spent time in the city doing what I wanted to do. In case my time was cut short and he fired me, for saying "ain't" or "ya'll" or "naw." I visited the Empire State Building, went to Rockefeller Center and the September 11th Memorial. That made me cry and my stomach felt sick. All those senseless deaths. I will never get over that. From there I visited the Metropolitan Museum of Art and walked through "the park." Central Park that is. I tried different food vendors and found that I enjoyed the hot dogs best of all.

Doing all of this alone wasn't as much fun as it had been with Ezra as my guide. I returned to the penthouse at the end of day two intending to order Chinese. Ezra was standing outside my door as if he were expecting me. And yes, he was still perfect. He couldn't make himself unattractive.

"Had a big day?" he asked smiling.

I nodded. "Yes. It was nice." I held up my bag from the art museum. I'd bought my sisters some souvenirs.

"Good. I thought I'd see if you wanted to have dinner. There's a Thai place you cannot miss. I go at least once a week."

I wasn't sure if I liked Thai or not, which meant I wanted to try it. I was lonely and spending the evening with Ezra sounded appealing to me.

"Sure, I'd like to eat Thai. I thought you'd be gone by now." I wondered why Ezra was in town if Hale wasn't in residence. He didn't appear to be a city kind of guy.

"I left when he did. And I'll leave in the morning. I came back for the Thai, my personal addiction, which keeps me away from others."

The look on his face said something else. Like maybe he was back for me. The idea made my heart race. I tried not to read into it. We had only one day and the kiss. I wasn't an expert at kissing, but it seemed like it was special.

"Okay, do I need to change?" I then walked to the door and pressed the code while waiting on his answer.

"You look perfect," he replied. "I prefer your clothes, but this isn't bad either, you make anything appear appealing."

I was wearing one of the casual outfits Hale had purchased for me. My limited wardrobe felt out of place and I didn't like looking unique. Especially while walking alone. Ezra's comment felt nice. My skin became tingly and warm. I couldn't keep from smiling at the man.

"Thank you. I'll put this bag in my room and we can go."

"Take your time. I'm in no rush."

I was hungry from all the walking. The hotdog I'd eaten wasn't enough. I needed more, but I didn't tell him that. I didn't want him to think I was ravenous, needed a trough or something.

"Where is it we're going?" I asked when I came back into the room. I hadn't taken the time to brush my hair or freshen up my face. I figured if I looked in the mirror I'd see a million little things I needed to fix and I was too hungry for that.

"It's called Uncle Boons. Not a big tourist spot, which is

always a win for me. Like I said the food is incredible. You can't get Thai food as good as Uncle Boons anywhere else in the states. I've tried and failed and haven't."

Uncle Boons didn't sound very Thai, but then how was I to know? I'd never eaten Thai in my life.

"Well, let's go try this place out."

"We'll need to take a cab from here. Walking would take an hour."

I hadn't taken a cab in the city. Flagging down a cab sounded fun. "Okay, I'm good with that."

"I don't do the fancy chauffeured shit like Hale does with his vehicles." It didn't sound like an apology. It was a statement without regret.

"I want to experience a New York cab," I honestly replied with excitement.

He chuckled at the comment. "God, you're a breath of fresh air. Didn't know I needed it until I walked into Hale's and you opened that mouth of yours."

My face flushed. I wanted to grin like an idiot because Ezra enjoyed my company as much as I did his. I really believed he'd come back to town just to see me in person. But I was afraid to think that thought. He could hurt me if I beamed it outward. No guy had ever had that kind of power over me. They'd all been from Moulton, Alabama. Sure, I'd been fooled by Hale and his wealth, but once I got to see him as he was, I realized he wasn't what I thought. He appeared to be more at first. Then I'd gotten here and he'd changed. This should concern me about Ezra. He could change just as quick. What was it he really wanted? And when had I gotten so dang jaded? Apparently I was hardening.

"Are you ever going to tell me about you? Where you're from, why you work with Hale? How about your last name?"

I was pushing but I needed some reassurance that he wouldn't vanish forever. Then I could safely let my heart get silly, if I knew he was coming back.

He was quiet for a while and I was preparing myself for Ezra not to respond. Finally he turned and there was a seriousness in his eyes that struck me deep within. Like he was alone and lost and abandoned.

"I lived another life in the past. One that is dead to me now. Dead to me, and everyone that I knew. To protect you I can't answer those questions. Matters can become what you don't want. And become that way really quick."

Thirty-Six

THAT WASN'T THE answer I'd expected. A dark and frightening response. Why would he need to protect me? Who was he? Who or what was Hale? I didn't respond as my mind raced and we left to hail a cab, the elevator closing behind us.

Getting in the iconic yellow taxi wasn't as exciting as it should've been. My thoughts weren't on the experience. They were replaying Ezra's words again and again in my head. How was his past life dead to him now? I didn't understand what he meant. I knew asking more questions would be pointless, he wouldn't respond if I did.

His hand slid over mine. I jumped, startled by the contact. "For tonight can you just forget about that? I leave in the morning and I've no idea when I'll get back to the city."

My chest ached when he spoke of leaving. I'd grown accustomed to having Ezra around. Being near him. Wanting to be with him. "Why do you have to go?" I asked, letting my emotions take hold, showing more than I should've permitted.

He sighed. "It's my job. I've done it for a long, long time."

That I understood. But the actual job scared the hell out of me. Nothing peaceful and safe could come from the answer he'd given in the elevator.

I tried to shake loose the foreboding that had settled in my chest like a worry. Like a fret that had no reason. I wanted to enjoy tonight. Ezra's answer didn't make me want him less.

"I can do that."

He squeezed my hand. "Thank you. It is greatly appreciated."

The cocky guy I'd met just last week hadn't turned out to be what I thought. I'd judged two men incorrectly. Hale and Ezra both in a row. I was beginning to think I sucked at first impressions and their meanings as it regarded me. That, or my dreams cloud my judgment. Dreams weren't a safe reality. Not when you wanted them so badly you didn't think them through. Hale was someone I thought Hale could never be and the worst kind of man imaginable. I'd come to New York to work for a monster, when his ultimate goal wasn't to hire me, but to groom me like a dog or a pony. Ezra then patiently spoke.

"I started working for Hale a year ago. What I do isn't important. But things aren't always what they seem and I need you to remember that."

I nodded. I didn't have to remember that. I'd just had that same revelation. Hale wasn't what he seemed. Now I had to make a decision to keep this dream or leave it and wait for the real one, though by leaving I'd lose Ezra. I wasn't sure I could do that. Unless he left and didn't return. Maybe this was the last thing we'd do together and then he'd vanish forever.

Before I made my decision I needed to find out what it was Hale did for a living. "I guess that means you can't tell me what it is Hale does with his time? He wasn't very open and direct about his actual job."

"That's because his 'actual job' is a gigantic goofy farce. His father gave him money and a title in his business. That's oil in Texas and Alaska, with a whole bunch of South American interests. Hale wanted more so he bought up other companies. Small businesses mostly, hotels and restaurants, and even a few old bars. He generally plays while his hirelings run it beneath his terrible gaze."

That was the most information I'd received from either of them thusfar.

"Yesterday he bought the bakery where your mother is employed. And yes, you can read into that. He didn't do it to improve her working conditions and he'll use it to lean on you. I'm breaking a rule by telling. You aren't supposed to know. Hale does nothing if it doesn't gain him something. He's not a giving man Sammy Jo."

My jaw dropped. He bought the bakery? "What could he possibly want with the bakery? He's not going to tear it down? My mother needs that job to live." Panic suddenly ate the rest of my emotions. The little bit of money I sent home wasn't going to meet their needs if she lost her job at the bakery.

"It won't change anything except maybe the owner. And like I said, it's to lean on you."

Frowning, I looked up at Ezra. "He won't be the owner?"

Ezra sighed. "He has no use for a bakery in Moulton, Alabama. But he does have a use for you. Giving your mother a bakery is his way of controlling the variables. Of buying you indirectly."

Oh.

I sat there torn between relief and fear. Mother wouldn't lose her job, but she might own the place because of him. If I made him happy by staying. If I became the 'Samantha' he desired.

"What have I done?" I whispered.

He didn't have a response. "For now, just continue as you are. Let him decide his next move. I'll know before you and I'll find you. We can then prepare your reaction."

This wasn't how I expected our night to go. But knowing I had Ezra on my side did help ease the fear. He seemed strong enough to help me. Ezra wasn't scared of Hale's power. I doubted he was scared of anyone. He had his own secrets I could never know, which should terrify and consume my interest, though they didn't, not in the least.

"Now you know the worst. Let's forget it and enjoy our night."

That couldn't be the worst. What I didn't know had to be worse than that. I knew that and he knew that I knew.

The cab stopped and Ezra handed him a twenty. "Keep the change," he said. He then opened his door to climb out. I took his hand and followed to the curb.

We were headed for the restaurant before I realized I hadn't even looked around, inside the cab or into the city. There was no memory to tuck away. The interior of the car or its details. My mind had been somewhere else. I didn't want my entire night to not be recalled in the future, because of what Ezra had told me. I wanted to enjoy his company. When would I see him again?

"I've never had Thai food, like I said."

"You like spicy food?" he asked.

I nodded and then I said "yessir."

"Then you'll love it. It can be the hottest."

I was sure Ezra was right. In Moulton the most exotic restaurant was an Italian place that served pizza. They had red-checkered table clothes and a limited pasta selection. There were candles on the tables with Italian music playing on the speakers, which set the mood. It was owned by a guy named Willy. Willy Joe who also worked as a welder. His wife Fanny ran the place.

The Thai restaurant was like an underground bar with colorful people and intriguing decorations and I forgot about my current predicament. I let myself soak it all in. Filed it away in my memory. It was another dream come true.

"I think you're right. I'm going to like this."

He squeezed my hand. "Love. You'll love it."

Thirty-Seven

THAI FOOD WAS different, but delicious. Ezra ordered a la carte and we shared five dishes because I couldn't make up my mind. The bottle of Pinot Gris that Ezra had ordered was good and worked well with the hotness. And once again I drank too much, though it was due to the spicy food.

I was giggling when we stepped from the cab to the street. Ezra had his arm around my waist. My hands and head didn't feel very steady and I couldn't walk without weaving. The whole shebang was hilarious to me.

"You're a light weight," he teasingly said.

"No, I'm just not a big drinker." I then stopped, hiccupped and laughed. "Normally I have moonshine punch at the barn dance once a year."

"Moonshine, huh? That's impressive."

I leaned into him as we walked off the elevator and approached Hale's front door. "It's not as yummy as the wine . . . moonshine isn't . . . actually it's not yummy at all. It tastes like burnt stream water, if that were even possible."

I laughed and he laughed too. "No, I guess it isn't yummy. What moonshine I've tasted was sour and harsh. But after a glass it got better. After two I forgot where I was."

I started to punch in the code. Ezra did it instead. How did he know the code? He'd never walked in before. Hale must trust him to give him those numbers with a kabillion expensive things waiting inside for the taking.

"You need a shower. I'll make a pot of coffee." He led me inside without mauling me. I'd heard stories but with him I felt safe.

I agreed a shower would feel wonderful. "Okay," I replied. "Good suggestion."

I started to walk away and then I changed my mind. I wanted a kiss again. The kind he'd given me before. If he was leaving I wanted something to remember. Was I the one mauling him?

Tripping to Ezra I grabbed both of his arms and stood on the tips of my toes, pressing my mouth to his own. He quickly wrapped his arms around me and I was glad for the support and embrace, otherwise I would've sprawled on the floor.

He didn't stop me, but instead, returned the kiss and let me taste the exotic food and wine still lingering on his tongue and in his mouth. I moaned, at least I thought I moaned, because Ezra didn't strike me as a moaner.

His hands scaled my spine in creeps until his thumbs were inches from my breasts. I wanted to arch my back so he could cover them both with his hands. Before I invited Ezra to continue he set me back away from his reach. I was cold and wanted his warmth.

When I opened my mouth to protest he raised an eyebrow and showed who he was. "You're drunk Sammy Jo and might regret it. As good as you feel and taste, I won't take advantage where I shouldn't. Your offer is sweet and sexy. And yes, I'd love to paw you, but I think I will pass till you're sober.

I should feel good about that. But I didn't, I felt frustrated.

With myself, because I'd drank too much. I wanted Ezra to do whatever he felt and I needed him to do it right now. Sammy Jo Knox was on the verge of begging. That's how aroused I was. I just referred to myself in third person. I must be losing my mind.

"Go get that shower," he said, nodding his head toward my room.

I didn't want to shower, unless he went with me, but I turned and did as he said. If I stayed in the room where I could see him I would rip off my clothes and plead. In the morning I had a feeling that would be embarrassing, though right now it seemed like heaven.

The water helped clear my head, as well as make me sleepy. I considered turning on the cold, but then vetoed that stupid idea. Thoughts of kissing Ezra danced through my head and I spent some extra time cleaning areas I knew he would touch and kiss. I was so well scrubbed that I glowed.

I dried off with a wrap around towel. My cotton sleep shorts and white tee shirt felt nice against my skin. I saw no reason to get dressed if he would be leaving soon. My bed looked nice and snug. Ezra would be gone tomorrow, so the bed would have to wait.

When I walked into the kitchen he poured a cup of coffee and extended his arm to me. "This will help, though actually it won't, drinking coffee drunk is a myth. Tap water and aspirin would be best. Coffee just seems more appropriate."

I took it, thanked him and sipped it. The blend was sweet and creamy, the way I liked it . . . and how the hell had he known how I liked it?

"It's perfect," I told him. "Am I that easy to read?"

He shrugged as if it weren't a big deal. "I'm just observant, though it's becoming a rarity. Most people never look around them."

Observant wasn't the description I had in mind, but I had to let it go and do it quickly.

"How was your shower? Feeling sober?"

I wanted to inform him of what I'd been doing. Then I didn't, but almost did. My God, it was like I was tracking him. Like hunting a wounded beast. "Nice. I'm better now." And still willing to get naked if you wish.

He glanced at his phone and grimaced. "Before I leave there's something I need to do. It's another sleepless night for me."

I didn't want him to go, thought we had all night, but apparently that was ending.

"Oh," I replied, wanting to beg, without managing to shame myself. My drunk must be wearing thin. I actually felt sense returning.

He took a step toward me, slid a finger under my chin and said "Sammy Jo, don't look so sad. It makes it hard to go and I have to. Work is calling me in."

I nodded and hoped he would kiss me. Give me something before walking away.

"I'll be back sooner than I planned. I can now admit that. You have my number if you need to call."

"Okay," I replied, feeling the excitement that Ezra would be returning.

"Jesus," he muttered, sliding his hand from my chin and into my hair. He then yanked me against his chest. We kissed, this time deeper, and maybe a little darker. Definitely, it was more intense. I did not want this to end. I did not want him to go. His job was important and ultimately I knew that his work had brought us together.

I soaked in his smell and the feel of his body. If he changed or I left and this didn't proceed I was sure this moment would remain special throughout my life. Ezra was extraordinary. A weird mix of contradictions. He was intense and intriguing, yet there was vulnerability in his eyes that didn't seem to fit. He was like a dog, a breed unto himself, who'd been hurt and couldn't trust. He shied away when you got close, but you knew he could eat you alive.

The words he'd spoken about his past before being dead haunted me and wouldn't relent. Did he truly mean them or were they meant to explain the severity of something he'd done?

He pulled away from me and shook his head. "You make it hard to leave."

I started to say "then don't." He anticipated my response, then put a finger directly on my lips.

"I have to go."

Again, I watched him leave. I wished I could join him to wherever he was going, but would I want to see what he did, once he reached his destination.

Thirty-Eight

THE WEEK PASSED by really slow. I saw some more sights, called home and talked to momma and my siblings were chatty and full of questions. Even Henry asked when he could see me, and that made me cry for a while. I talked to Jamie about her pregnancy, which was making her really ill, though Ben was being great about it. From her stories about the vomiting I decided that a baby wasn't for me until later. Much, much, much, much, much later. Momma had never complained carrying Henry. I wouldn't have known if she was sick. She hid the sickness and never said a thing. Jamie was different, softer, not tough, and I was guessing that was generational. My mother was incredibly durable. But loving just the same.

I almost texted Ezra twice then stopped myself before I did. I wasn't drunk anymore and remembered I was raised not to chase boys or men. If he wanted to talk to me he'd get in touch when he could and had the time. And I was wishing that time was now. I looked at my phone a million times a day to see if he'd texted or called. That was pathetic and I knew it. I did it anyway, because the man had pulled me in and I couldn't quit thinking about him.

By the time day seven rolled around I was mad as hell at him. He'd not called or texted. It was as if last week hadn't happened. I didn't like games and this felt like a game and I wasn't going to play. If he called I wasn't answering. His window had passed and he'd failed.

I hadn't studied for Hale's parties like he said I should because what was I supposed to study? He'd been vague and assumed I knew what he meant. I was aware I didn't know my proper social graces, but how could a website help me? Was I supposed to sit manikins around a big table and pretend to entertain them?

I watched people from that world, or what I assumed were from that world, while touring around the city. They had a polished look about them. One you couldn't miss when you stared. That was my course so far.

Hale would return in a week. Would Ezra return when he did? I hoped so and that made me pathetic. I couldn't drive the man from my head. I was trying to stay focused on other things, but Ezra's absence was driving me nuts.

Jamie had asked me about Hale and myself. I explained that he was my employer and I his employee. It was that and nothing more. But I hadn't told her about Ezra. It was a secret and I didn't know why, other than he worked with Hale. Deep down I was protecting Ezra. I knew that was important to the both of us because Hale had become unpredictable. I never knew what the man would do.

I tugged my reusable grocery bag up onto my shoulder. I turned the corner and headed for the penthouse. My thoughts were everywhere and with them worry. I'd lost interest in the world around me. The scenes I'd craved and adored. I then came back to the people in the streets, blocking my thoughts and concerns. There was a mother strolling with her baby. A man on his phone in a suit. An older woman pushed her walker down the street and then there was, what, there was Ezra? With a tall, leggy brunette. They were close and whispering as if they'd something important to discuss between themselves. It was intimate, well, I think so, intimate enough to cause anger.

I paused and put them in focus. Sure enough it was Ezra. I hadn't dreamed him up because I was missing his company. That was Ezra, here in New York. With a woman I didn't know.

If I were brave I would approach. Walk over to the couple and pretend as if seeing them was a nice surprise. Just so he'd know I saw him. He was here and close and the man had ignored me, after doing and saying what he did.

But I wasn't brave or even stealthy. I wanted to sneak past them and get to the penthouse one block down from this street. After that I'd forget I saw him and eventually try to disremember I threw myself on his charm and good looks. Of course he had other women. He was beautiful, dangerous, and intriguing. I was silly to think I was special. Or that our kiss meant something to him.

I wondered if she'd been "the work" he rushed off to the other night. He was completely into me and then he wasn't and . . . no, she could be his wife! My stomach knotted and I felt sick. Was he married? Oh God, what if he was married? That would make me an adulterer! Momma would be ashamed. Not as much as I was ashamed of myself.

I crossed the street and stepped into a bookstore. I could see them, but they couldn't see me. I'd wait until they moved down the block before I left and returned to the penthouse. Facing him was impossible right now. He might be married or engaged. What if he was engaged? Was that as terrible as being married? Either way I'd become "the other." The other woman in Ezra's scheme.

Conquering the world single was sounding more and more appealing. Men couldn't be trusted. They wanted women. Lots of women. One woman would never be enough. Women craved that sole connection. A man who would love them eternally. Right now it appeared that men wanted sex and the better the variety and distance between them the more sex they could have without caring. I knew my daddy was precious. I wish more males would behave like him. He was a decent caring individual. I'd set my goal too high.

I watched from the window as I pretended to look at a cookbook about barbecuing, which I'd never actually attempt. The woman was close to Ezra. Looking serious as she spoke and gestured. Like they were discussing something important. Her skirt couldn't be any shorter. If she bent over you'd see her vagina and for crying out loud she was hot.

Although they weren't embracing or showing affection, their bodies were close and familiar. There was something between them, I was sure about that, but just what it was seemed vague.

Finally she said something, squeezed his arm affectionately, before turning and strutting away, her stiletto heels clicking and tiny skirt grabbing, although he didn't watch her go. That was surprising to me. She was shaking her ass for him to enjoy, but he threw his attention to the street, musing on some other thing.

Crap, he was headed toward the penthouse. I wasn't going to be there waiting like a good little girl for his pawing. I knew better now. I was hardening.

Once he was out of sight I left the bookstore and reversed my trek, went back the way I had come. I knew a good food vendor three blocks away and I could take my food to the park and eat it while staking the penthouse. He'd give up and leave I bet. Why waste his time waiting on me when he had legs waiting on him.

I decided I hadn't missed anything in life by not dating the guys in Moulton. Other than Ben there were no good guys. For all I knew Ben was the same. He could be out dilly-dallying other woman while Jamie threw up in a sink. The idea made me even angrier. If I found out he was I'd go to Moulton to stomp his butt. Stupid, stupid men!

A whistle startled me and I turned to see a creeper checking my walk and ogling. He was working on a building in a hardhat. He winked and waggled his tongue. I then channeled my frustration, flipped my middle finger, and with a snarl I stalked off. This life was increasing my harshness. I didn't care. I needed it to. Being naïve wasn't healthy. It led to dumb decisions and heartache. I'd already had enough of both.

Thirty-Nine

WHILE OPENING THE door to the penthouse part of me wondered if I'd see Ezra waiting on the other side. I knew he could get in when he wanted. What I didn't expect was to see Hale there with a glass of amber liquid and a scowl painted on his face. I was dressed in his clothing. The apartment was clean. I was allowed to leave, was I not? Why was he angry with me?

"Hello," I said, hearing the crack in my voice, realizing I was holding my breath.

He glared with disapproval. I felt my hands begin to sweat. I raced through all his reasons for annoyance but what it was seemed lost to me.

"Have you spoken to your mother today?"

That was his question. Had I talked to my momma? No. Not today. I shook my head. "Is she okay?"

He then cocked an eyebrow at me. "I'd say so. She now owns the bakery. I bought it and gave it to her. Do you know why I did that Samantha?"

To control me Hale. To own me. To create a wall of guilt. Ezra had told me as much. I just hadn't been sure he was right. Now seeing the look on Hale's face I wondered if he'd been correct.

"No," I honestly replied.

He took a drink and his mouth held its hard line. "It was a gift to you. You said you wished your mother could own a bakery. Now your mother does."

Oh well, that was nice.

"Thank you, that's a generous gift. I don't know what to say exactly." Because I didn't believe he had done it. Buying me a gift like that made no sense at all. Unless there were strings attached. What was the price I would pay?

"How about starting by telling me where you've been all day. I arrived at noon and you weren't here. It's after eight and you're just coming home. I've wasted an entire day waiting on you and I'm not very happy about it."

He wasn't due for another week. "I was out exploring the city. Then I got food from a vendor and ate it in the park. Why didn't you call me Hale?" I thought that was a decent question. One that made sense to ask. His scowl then deepened and I suddenly realized I wasn't supposed to ask questions in his presence.

"I shouldn't have to call my employee and ask her why she isn't working."

"But I left everything clean." I immediately defended myself.

"Does that mean you've completed your other assignment? You're ready to submerge in my world. I doubt that highly Samantha."

No, I wasn't ready. I didn't want to "submerge" in his world. I'd rather "submerge" into a sewer system.

"I've been studying but I'm not prepared."

He sat his glass on the table and it almost shattered. I jumped and my heart began racing.

"I bought your mother a bakery Samantha, because you wished it and now it is hers. And in return I get you running around the city taking advantage of me, the life I provide, and does that sound fair to you?"

Was he actually becoming a victim? After purchasing a friggin' bakery? He made it sound like I was using him. That wasn't how this was at all. "I was watching the people in the city. I can't learn shut inside this apartment." The expression on his face was frightening. I was fairly sure he wouldn't hurt me. Hale was just upset. "I'm sorry. I thought I had another week. I wanted to walk around. It was lonely being in here."

He snarled and my eyes went wide. Hale's face then contorted into some weird mask forcing me to retreat. I took three steps back and stopped. There was danger in his eyes and voice. This was why Ezra wanted me to call him. His warning was now before me.

"Lonely?" he replied, taking a step in my direction while cracking his knuckles and scowling. "You, Sammy Jo Knox, were lonely in the big ol' city? The girl who wanted nothing more than to escape her hick town full of what she referred to as 'permanents'? She then manages a penthouse in greedy Manhattan and complains about being lonely. Can you not afford to be happy? Are you already that spoiled and demanding, that you require constant attention?"

"That's not what I meant Hale." My voice sounded like that of a child. I was scared and it was obvious. He was wrong on every point.

"It's how you're acting Samantha. You aren't grateful for one damn thing. Do you know the girls who would promise their souls to be in your shoes at this moment? What they'd give up to live here? To be on my arm at those parties? Do you? No, of course not. You're goofy and simple minded. All you know is the country ass life you've lived and I tell you, the world isn't basic.

Not one fucking bit my dear."

This wasn't getting any better. I was making it worse with every word that I said, so I did what I knew was safe. "I'm sorry Hale. Please forgive me." It was an apology I didn't mean, but I said it anyway.

He let loose a laugh and remarked. "You're sorry?" he said, shutting the distance, as the fury flashed in his eyes. Why was Hale so angry? He had no reason to be. The man was a psychopath. "I don't care if you're fucking sorry. I care that you get your stupid ass educated and learn proper behavior. I own you Samantha Knox. You have the innocent beauty that will ideally fit on my arm in the public sphere. I knew that the moment I saw you. That's why you are here. To be exactly what I need you to be. You do as I say and you don't make decisions for yourself ever again. Do I make myself clear? Is it crystal?"

I was stunned. I just stood there. His words had left me empty. This wasn't what I'd come for. I never agreed to being a piece of property. "I didn't ask you to buy my mother the bakery . . ." I managed to get that out before his hand struck my face. I flew against the door I'd come through, the distance the length of my body and my jaw was on fire with pain.

"Ungrateful bitch!" he roared. His voice was deranged and cultured Hale was gone from the city and the planet. My vision was blurry and my nose was bleeding as I tried to hold myself up. I needed to get my footing to defend against his coming onslaught. If I was down he might kill me.

My head was screaming RUN when he grabbed my arm and twisted it unnaturally behind me. I cried in pain, the muscle was tearing, and I was sure he would snap a bone.

"Shut up! I didn't say you could fucking speak! I'm tired of hearing your voice!" And with that he slammed me against the door twice, causing my head to bounce. I blinked, but the world was still blurry. I wanted to cry and beg him to stop, but was afraid of what he'd do if I spoke and made any noise.

"You wanted this life. I MADE it happen. I've spent hundreds of thousands of dollars making your life what you dreamed. You expect me to want nothing in return? Are you that stupid, you bitch? I didn't do it for fucking free. You'll conform to what I want or you'll pay me back every dime."

Pay him back? Why would he expect that? My head was splitting open from the pain and my arm was still twisted behind me. It was hard to breathe with the panic. I would say whatever I needed to say in order to get him away. Then I would run straight home. I could afford the bus. I wasn't staying here. This was enough for me.

"I don't waste time Samantha. I get what I want when I want it. Do you understand that? Is it clear? You will do what I fucking say."

I couldn't answer. My ability to speak was stolen by the horror of his terror. He jerked my arm and threw me again off the door and I landed on the floor with a whump. "Talk now woman! Speak! You have my motherfucking permission!"

I opened my mouth while praying in my head that I could say anything to stop him. One syllable to make him quit. As my words were forming the door swung inward and there was something else in the room. Another presence I couldn't make out.

Forty

"BACK AWAY FROM her Hale. Do it now." Ezra's voice was a welcomed sound. The tears that had pooled in my eyes ran freely down my cheeks. He was here. I wasn't going to die.

"Go check on her," he said to another and there was someone else beside me. With the blow to my head my vision was bad and I couldn't see who it was. She was then on her knees beside me gently touching my face. It was the woman from the street earlier in the day. The female I'd seen with Ezra. I didn't want her hands on my body, but I had no strength to resist her.

"She needs a doctor," the woman told him, with concern in her voice and manner.

"What the fuck are you doing Hale? You assault women now as a hobby?" The anger was clear in his voice. Hale was only mildly concerned.

"Ezra, you work for me. Don't question my decisions or actions and never barge into my house." Hale replied without emotion in his voice. As if talking about the weather.

"I work for your father, not you. That's who I fucking work for. And he wouldn't be okay with you beating a woman you entitled little prick." Ezra's tone had gone from angry to a barely controllable fury.

"No sir, you work for me." After he replied his body turned towards me. He motioned with his hand for the woman to move and spoke as if I were nothing. "Move back. She doesn't need a doctor. You're creating drama that doesn't need to be. You will both do what I say."

Ezra was holding words in his mouth that had never been spoken before. He knew something Hale did not know and would not unless Ezra informed him. And so Ezra said it like this: "you could possibly be the target of a hit. Your father hired me to protect you. As for her, she's leaving with us and I'm getting her medical attention."

Either my brain was a mess from the beating or I was hearing that Ezra was security. A bodyguard hired for Hale. Why would Hale need protecting? He seemed capable enough.

"What hit?" Hale asked, his tone then changing to something else entirely. He wasn't unconcerned anymore.

"Ah, now that it centers on your precious existence your attitude suddenly shifts. Business gone bad my man. I think you probably know more about it than you want to admit," said Ezra. "Now I'm taking Sammy Jo to a doctor. You call your father and figure this out."

Hale stepped between Ezra and I. "She's not leaving. She's fine. Nothing is permanent. She's roughed up but will survive. You both can leave and pack your bags because once I talk to my father you'll each be out of a job."

Ezra laughed then yanked it back. It was a deep twisted laugh like the man was amused because Hale had to tell his father to have any power at all.

"Can you take a deep breath?" she asked me. The woman was talking quietly to me and the concern in her voice was motherly. As much as I didn't want my focus off the others I glanced at her instead. She was even more beautiful up close. And she was truly worried about me. It was hard to hate someone who was trying to help you and meant it.

I nodded and winced. "Just sore. My chest and neck hurt a little."

She frowned and looked at Ezra. "We need to take her now."

"We will," Ezra replied. "Hale, I'll put it like this. Move or you're going through the sheetrock. I will put you through that wall."

I expected Hale to refuse. He then cleared and backed away. "Do what you want. You're all three fired and that goes for your mother Samantha. I'm closing the bakery and selling the building. Then your family can starve to death and it will be your fault."

Ezra didn't say anything. He stalked past Hale, bent down in front of me and asked "Sammy Jo, what hurts? Don't leave any place out."

"Mostly my face, head and arm," I replied in a childish whisper. "I'm sorry, no, it's my body. He kept . . ."

"You don't have to say another word." Ezra slid his arms under my knees and back and lifted me as if I were weightless.

"You're both going to regret this," Hale said. We then left the penthouse with the woman following, spinning to see what he'd do. She slammed the door with force and then stood there, listening for movement behind it. "God, I wish we could be fired. I hate that spoiled little bitch. We should leave 'em a gap to knock his ass off and then act like we didn't know." Apparently she was something else. And she sounded mean as hell.

"His father will deal with him." Ezra replied businesslike. "Go ahead and call him please. Give him a run down of what's happened to date. He'll have heard all of this and he will need an update. Then stay close to the place and watch who comes and goes. I'll update you on Sammy Jo as soon as we get where we're going. Use your second phone and not the first whenever you speak with his father. Then switch back to the first. You know what to do."

"Got it," she responded to the order. She was happy to receive it and did so.

I stared up at Ezra then back at her. The woman was glaring at the floor numbers as they flashed in the descending elevator. "I swear I hate that bastard," she muttered.

Ezra nodded in agreement. Then he looked down at me. "How're you feeling? A little less stress?"

"Like she got her ass beat," the woman replied. "Don't make her talk if she doesn't have to."

Ezra ignored her and watched me closely.

I told him "sore and more than confused."

His frown then deepened and "we should've come sooner. I didn't realize he was hurting you. The last time you cried out I knew he had."

"What are you?" I asked still wondering. Was I unconscious in the apartment and dreaming all of this. Were Ezra and the woman not real? Not my current reality?

"I'm what I told Hale I was. And yes, this is actually happening. I'm protecting him for his father. There's been a business deal go bad in South America concerning one of his interests. He believes they'll go after Hale, being as that's his only son. Hale knew nothing about it. His father didn't want to concern him. He believed I was working for him. Now for the introduction."

"I'm Gia. I work for Ezra." The woman said it and smiled and flashed her eyes and it even made my wounded heart leap. He had a hot female employee? Great. That's just perfect. All girls want to know the guy they like has a porn star working in their care. "Oh," was all I could say. I should tell her thanks for helping me but my jealousy was plainly ridiculous. I'd be going back to Moulton. I'd never see Ezra or this Gia again and I would have to find a job to help momma. My dream was gone. It was finished. It went from dreamy to weird to a nightmare and I had to get free of its grip.

The elevator opened and Ezra left Gia inside while he carried me out. There was a black car waiting for us. The driver opened the door and Ezra climbed inside with me folded in his arms like a chair. This wasn't Hale's car or driver. I thought Ezra didn't do black cars.

"Whose car is this?"

"It's Christopher's. Hale's father first name is Christopher. I had to tell him I was taking you from Hale. He immediately sent the car. He heard everything that was said in the apartment. I was wired as he requested."

This all had to be a dream. I had to be unconscious in Hale's apartment sound asleep while rolling through this. That made sense to me. I just hoped I didn't die.

Forty-One

THOUGH THIS WASN'T a dream and I wasn't catatonic, because the IV the nurse was trying to administer wasn't agreeing with my vanishing veins. The digging of the needle couldn't be non-reality and neither was my splitting headache. Yes, this was all happening. And it got even more confusing. Ezra, who was standing beside me, was security for the rich and the spoiled? Was that why he was so secretive? And why was his helper a female? Wouldn't a man do a better job? Apparently I knew very little. And that was getting smaller and smaller.

"Sorry. We got it this time." The nurse smiled apologetically for having to stick me three times to get a good vein. "We'll start the fluids first then deal with the pain. What he prescribed is on its way. When she brings it I'll give you a dose."

"Thank you," I replied. "I appreciate it." She said "you're welcome," then looked at Ezra, with suspicion and what you'd call angst. She didn't appear to trust him. They'd asked me what had happened and I told them that my boyfriend beat me up. Ezra had coached me on this and the details of what would happen. If I said my employer then lawyers and policemen would immediately get involved. I'd have to deal with them. I didn't want all that scrutiny. Inciting any more anger from Hale wasn't appealing to me.

"Are you okay if I step out a moment?" the nurse asked rather straightforwardly. She didn't completely believe my story.

"Ezra's who saved me. Not who hurt me," I repeated again and again.

She nodded and replied "okay." She left the room staring at Ezra.

"She doesn't believe me," I said. I then turned my head and frowned. I was on the verge of tears.

"They get a lot of domestic abuse. I'm sure this hallway has other cases. She's just being careful. I'm not insulted Sammy Jo. She should be suspiciously pissed. Boys shouldn't hit girls."

I closed my eyes and said nothing further. That helped somewhat with the pain. My skull felt like a vice was clamped on it and the handle was being spun.

"I should've come in sooner. I knew it would eventually happen." His hand touched my forehead and brushed my hair back. He was a gentle but ferocious man.

"You came in when it was needed. You had no way to know. Ezra, you can't see through walls. I'm going to be okay." I was too tired to keep reassuring him. But I did have a question or two: "is Gia your girlfriend? Are you getting married? Or is she already your wife in secret?" There, I covered it all. Time for the truth I guess.

Ezra chuckled. "No and no and no. She has her own girlfriend. The same one for the past five years. She has zero interest in me. Or any other man as that goes."

Girlfriend? Oh, she's a lesbian. That's not at all what I was expecting.

"Gia was a Marine. Gia's mental and physical evaluations scored the same or better than the males. Not the bottom rung, but the top. She's not really a human." He laughed and then he held it. "I don't completely understand her myself. She gets the job done and is more efficient than most men in this particular business. They wouldn't hire her because she's a woman. I hired her before ten other men and none of them have taken a bullet. Gia's taken three. One still sits near her spine."

I hadn't been that nice to her. She could twist my head from my shoulders. I felt guilty now. She'd shown she cared and I was harsh. My jealousy kept me from being grateful.

"I need to apologize. Will I ever see her again?"

"Why do you need to apologize?" Although my eyes were closed, I could tell he was smiling.

"Because I was jealous and possessive of you. I saw the two of you earlier on the street and I thought, well, you know."

This time Ezra roared. "Gia doesn't need or expect an apology. She would've killed Hale a thousand times over if she wouldn't have been in my employment."

That didn't matter. She deserved one. "I should've been nicer to her."

The sound of the door interrupted us. "Pain medicine is here," the nurse sang. She sounded chipper and fairly upbeat.

"It'll be cold," she said. She then picked up my hand and administered the dosage directly through my IV. The sensation in my veins only lasted a minute and then the air became greasy and I drifted off into space.

"Nighty night," Ezra said.

When I came to there were voices in the room. Two men, gruff and masculine. I kept my eyes closed and listened.

"You need to get her home. She's not safe with him. You knew that from the beginning. I thought you'd learned your lesson. You can't get attached to a woman while working a job."

Ezra released a hard laugh. "As if you can talk. You're married to Nan."

Who was Nan? What the hell? Was I dead? No, that was Ezra.

"I left the business. You, however died, so you could live this life. It was what you wanted my friend. Dead men can't have relationships. They can't care for another like this."

Dead? He wasn't dead. Was I still asleep?

"I know what I can and can't do. Cope, Jesus, back off. I shouldn't have called you to help."

"But you did. Now deal with my opinion. It is now in the fucking room."

Ezra sighed. "Just get her home safe. Let me know when she's there if you will. I don't trust anyone else. Not with her I don't. Hale's father was right from the start. He's a fucked up piece of shit. There are things going on that Hale doesn't know and the water is over his head. It's about to get bad, then worse. She needs to stay away from him."

"I'll get her there safe. I promise. But I don't do this shit anymore. I've got to get home to Nan and Axel, they're waiting and expecting me. Because she doesn't know that you aren't dead I couldn't tell her the truth about this. I'm not getting sucked back in."

"Understood. I owe you one." Ezra replied sounding humble.

"No Major, you owe me a fucking ton, this just adds to your tally."

Major? Who was Major?

"Whatever. Just get her home. I've got to go to Tennessee and deal with this. Christopher is waiting on me."

"Go ahead. This is taken care of."

I wanted to open my eyes and beg him not to leave. But I didn't for several reasons. Ezra was supposed to be dead. There was a strange man calling him Major and this Major had to go to Tennessee. I'd been a part of his work, this Ezra-Major, though

Ezra didn't exist. What had I gotten myself into?

Moulton had been a prison. Now it was where I wanted to be. Life was simple there. People were real. This life wasn't for me. The price was too high and I wouldn't pay it, so I kept my eyes closed and waited until Ezra was gone and the stranger followed. Once I knew I was alone I stared at the wall in the room and there was comfort. Peace in returning to Moulton. Soon I'd be home to rebuild a life I'd completely turned upside down, by leaving the town in the first place. The security of the bakery was no longer. But I would be there to help. We would be okay, every one of us. As a family we would survive.

Forty-Two

I NEVER SAW the man. The one whose voice I heard in the room. Instead, Gia came to stay. When they released me the following day I had a brace on my arm. Ligaments were torn but the vomiting had stopped and my concussion was on the mend. Gia took me to the airport. She had all my things from the penthouse. I assumed Hale gave them over. He wouldn't say no to her. That might get you thrown from the balcony.

She begged me to eat while we waited on my plane. However, when it was time to leave, she didn't go, although she had a ticket. "I'm headed to Tennessee," she said with a smile and a pat. "You'll be fine Sammy Jo. You may think you're alone but you're not."

Then she walked away.

I glanced around at the people boarding and wondered if he was here. The man who was escorting me. Observing my return to Moulton. Why couldn't I know who he was? Had he been following us all this time?

The safety and security of a simple life in Moulton had never sounded more appealing. This world I was in right now was far bigger and scarier than I'd imagined. It wasn't the answer to my hopes and dreams. Wasn't all lights and excitement. It was dark and twisted, with an abundance of shadows and my soul wouldn't be sold, not to become something else.

Stepping into line I bumped into a man and turned to tell him I was sorry. I had to tilt my head back to see him. He was tall with a beard and a man bun. His eyes were beautiful and I had a feeling without that beard he was gorgeous. The wall of muscle on his frame made me nervous. Before Hale men hadn't frightened me. Now every size and shape caused a panic. Especially larger males.

"I'm sorry," I said quickly.

"My fault," was his short reply. He didn't smile or make eye contact. He glanced down at his phone then back at the line and his breathing was deep and steady. His chest rose and fell like the sea.

I turned and focused on the line as it slowly moved forward. The purse my mother had made me was locked on my shoulder and the clothes I wore were mine. Moulton was at the end of the day.

The life Hale had afforded was behind me. I had a few fond memories, though they weren't with Hale, they were exclusively with Ezra in the city. He'd found a way into my heart and I couldn't believe I would never see Ezra again. He was the guy I'd dreamed as a child. Yet I knew nothing about him. Because of his job Ezra was a lie. I didn't know his true identity. That saddened me to an extreme. When he'd explained to me that his former life was dead, it was and Ezra was serious. He wasn't exaggerating. His "before" was a different person. Never again would we laugh over dinner, or drink too much at a restaurant. Ending the night with a toe-curling kiss was now an unrepeatable memory. I'd been given a taste of what a real man was and then it was snatched from my grasp. Nothing I could do would get it back. I'd never been in his future plans. He was working when he spent time with me. It was a ruse, a fake and a con.

My seat on the plane was in first class. The big man sat beside me. Striking eyes and bun still there. He didn't speak or glance my way. Instead he ordered a whiskey from the flight attendant and I ordered a soda after that. I didn't try and talk because he gave off the vibe he wasn't into conversation.

The rest of the flight was the same. The man beside me finished his drink and closed his eyes to rest. I turned my attention to the window. As we rose in the sky the clouds covered then cleared. This was my second time on a plane and it would be my last. I wasn't chasing this dream again. I didn't need another adventure. I wanted family, security and home. Maybe love would arrive one day. If I could learn to trust what brought it.

I no longer had a phone to call home. Momma didn't know I was coming. I wondered if Hale got in touch with her. What would he tell her if he did?

Calling her from the hospital had been out of the question. It would've scared her and I'd done enough. I'd changed her life by coming to New York and now her life was altered again and my family was upside down. All because of me.

My momma was the best in the state of Alabama. Nobody could cook like her. She loved people enjoying her products. I'd taken that away from her. There wasn't another bakery in Moulton. She wouldn't be able to find another job where she ran it and made it prosper, because the customers wanted her treats.

I had to make it up to her. I would work three jobs if needed. She could stay home with Henry and I would take care of things. I'd save and work and buy her a bakery. It'd take years but I would do it. I owed her that because of my selfishness.

The pilot spoke and said we'd be landing soon. The flight had seemed fast, but of course I knew my thoughts had been elsewhere. I had to prepare to face my family. The pressure was mine to deal with.

I would be landing in Huntsville and I wondered how I was supposed to get to Moulton. I had some money but a bus didn't go there. If Gia hadn't planned a car or a ride I was going to call someone. Jamie and Ben would be best. I could pay for their gas and time. I had enough money for that. I didn't want to bother momma. She was currently losing her job. That was my fault, not hers.

After the plane landed I retrieved my purse from under the seat in front of me. The man beside me slid my carry on from the compartment and calmly handed it down.

"Thank you," I said and he nodded, remaining silent, saying nothing.

Something about him was peaceful. When you first looked at him he was large and intimidating, but there was a way about his demeanor. It eased you being next to him. There wasn't any anger or hostility. Under the surface he did not seethe. That's the best way to explain it.

When allowed to exit the plane he stepped back and let me go first. I went ahead and although I wanted to thank him I knew he didn't expect it. I headed for the gate to find a bank of phones, if those even existed in this airport. Cell was king, even I knew that.

"Good luck," the deep voice said. It came from behind me and I surprisingly turned because it was him speaking to me. He then vanished into the crowd as if he'd never been.

While redirecting my attention to the busy airport my gaze stopped on my mother. She was amongst a bunch of people but seeing her face made my eyes fill with tears. Her expression was full of relief and love and that tenderness she'd always given. I then saw forgiveness, which made me grow calm. "Mother, there was my mother." I was home and safe with her. I should've never left Moulton to begin with. Not one tear had threatened to fall since the world I'd chosen began to crumble and then it crumbled around me. The little girl that I was, and that every woman is, fell to pieces in her presence. She'd bend down to pick them up. That's what a mother did.

Forty-Three

"NO NEED TO cry. It's time to toughen up. It went to pieces and we'll adjust. The world ain't ended. Still spinnin'. We got our health and we got each other." Those were momma's words and as they sank in I threw myself into her arms. She was strong but I started to cry. That was always comforting knowing momma wasn't scared when we, her children, were. She wasn't afraid of anything. If there was anyone in this world I wanted to be like it was her, my mother and my friend.

"I'm sorry," I sobbed, tried to pull myself together, while she patted my back and kissed my temple.

"I know. But you live and learn and I had to let you do this. It's the way we grow up and mature."

I sniffled and squeezed her tightly. She'd expected me to return in a similar condition, because she knew fairytales were limited. You only got so far and then they changed.

"Now tell me, how bad are you hurt?" She pulled back to have a look at me.

She knew I was injured and she knew to be here. I wondered

if Ezra or Major, or whoever he was had called. "Who told you I was coming?"

Momma shrugged, "I honestly don't know. Some woman. Said you'd been beaten. She told me Hale did the damage and that she and her partner rescued you from his penthouse. She gave me your arrival information. That was it. Nothing more."

Gia. I hoped I saw her again. I owed her an apology and a thank you. But I knew she was gone forever. That part of my life was over. Ezra, Gia and New York were finished. My chest ached from the thought as I fought back tears. I needed a life in a place that was safe. If common and boring, okay, at least I would have my family.

"Let's go home," I said. Momma then squeezed my arm. The good one, not the other.

"The horde can't wait to see you. They've missed you to the point of insanity."

As she told me we began walking towards the exit. My mind was churning with energy.

"I'll start job hunting tomorrow. I'll get three jobs if I have to."

She frowned. "Why would you do that? You can work at the bakery with the others. Lordy Sammy Jo, there's space."

The bakery? The others? Momma didn't know. My stomach felt sick and flipped. She wasn't aware that the bakery was about to be closed and sold. How was I supposed to tell her? She hadn't had time to prepare for this and think about what to do. I was a terrible daughter. I'd ruined her.

"Momma," I replied with sadness. I wished I could do it again. Go back a month and make it right. "The bakery is being closed and the building will be sold. Hale told me that before I left."

Momma didn't pause or stop walking. I was unsure my mother had heard me. "Hale junior believed that would happen. But I received word this morning that Christopher Hale Jude number two, Hale's father and a really nice fella, has bought the bakery and it will remain open. I am in charge and will continue to be. Your sisters are working there now. Mr. Jude's new capital he put into the business made room for employees. You should see Henry's little area. He can play and entertain himself."

This was Ezra's doing. I kept quiet. Momma wasn't ready to hear about Ezra. He'd made an impact and then he was gone. Letting him go was going to be painful and I hoped over time it got easier. Right now it didn't seem like it would. I knew he had secrets, unimaginable darkness, that I could never want to understand. I would always miss him and wonder what if. What if it would've been us? That, by itself, is a beautiful thing. A sad, though a beautiful thing.

"I didn't need to own a bakery. When I got the news from Hale that he'd bought it, I was upset and really angered. I didn't want a gift like that. That there is an unpardonable burden. I knew it was to control you and that made me sick. Not owning that place is a relief. I love to bake, and if I could buy it, that would be a different story. But I don't want a man buying me shit. I can do it myself."

"I'm sorry, so sorry I went. I beg your forgiveness for this." I knew that my choices still affected everyone and that they were worried and sick about me.

"Sammy Jo, we all make mistakes. It's part of growing up and learning. What matters is that we remember those mistakes and don't make the same ones twice. It'll toughen you up and God knows you need that. Sometimes a head in the clouds gets rained on."

The first real smile I'd felt in days touched my lips and spread to my face. Momma always knew the right thing to say to keep me from falling apart. She was blunt but encouraging and it came in a package that was wrapped with a ribbon of love.

"That pretty face of yours is a little banged up but it'll heal and life will go on. Other men will come and go. Then one day the right one will collide and everything will change in an instant. You'll know it's real and there won't be a fairytale attached to what he offers. He will make you smile, feel secure and safe, the best friend you've ever had. That's when you know it's right. It's what I had with your daddy. No man will ever take his place. He's gone, but the time I spent with the man are the very best years of my life. Know that you will also find that. Waiting on him is the most important part. Soul mates ain't ordered and registered."

The entire time she was talking I saw Ezra's picture in my mind. I'd felt all those things with him, yet he wasn't the right one because he was impossible to know or get close to. He lived a life devoid of real human contact. The only reason I felt safe with him was that making you safe was his job. He guarded the rich and famous. I hoped the man momma was talking about would find me in Moulton, Alabama. However, I doubted that.

We walked to her car and put my luggage inside then headed home off the main roads. Back to the bedroom I shared with my sisters. Back to my friends who were expecting a baby and living the married life. Back to the bakery, where I would sell sweets, to the people in town who knew me. Back to everything I thought I hated.

And I couldn't wait to get there.

The only memories I had of New York City that I could replay in my head at night were those I spent with Ezra. He was gone but in my heart I could visit him. One day I wouldn't think about him and I could move on from those thoughts.

"What if you think you've fallen in love, but it's an impossible situation?" I was unable to bite my tongue. I had to ask her and so I did.

"If it's real Sammy Jo, it's possible."

Explaining to her what I meant was completely out of the question. She couldn't know about Ezra. Now I was protecting him and I didn't even know why. Didn't know what from or if my secrecy did him any good at all.

"But what if it isn't?" I asked, unable to let it go.

"If it's real then life will open the right path. You just have to wait. Time will tell."

I could wait but I knew waiting was in vain. I closed my eyes and laid my head back. My memories would have to be sufficient. Until those memories would fade.

Forty-Four

*H*AZEL WAS WAITING in the yard before the car could even stop. As she ran in circles her long curly hair flew up into the air like antlers, the smile on her face whitely beaming. I felt my eyes fill with tears and realized how much I'd missed them. More so than I had imagined. Hazel's excitement made life whole. For a moment I was complete.

"She's missed you the most, that one there. I'd say she's gone insane with the gigglies." Momma said it to be touching and it was.

"I missed her crazy myself," I replied. As soon as we stopped I opened the door and Hazel pinned me to the seat, her arms clutched tightly around my neck. She held on as I gently forced her back.

"Sammy Jo," she squealed, like a young girl squeals. "I'm so glad you're home forever!"

So was I. Right now forever was fine with me, and the bakery seemed like heaven.

"I also missed you precious." I told her with a smile on my face that eased some of my pain. I carefully positioned my arm so her excitement couldn't injure me further. She pulled back and a frown touched her lips. "Your face is hurt Sammy Jo."

"I told you she was slapped around. But she's fine. Be gentle with her. Especially her arm," said momma.

Hazel loosened her grip. "I forgot. Are you okay?"

"I'm fine. Much better now." I then hugged her to me with my good arm.

"Ohmygod you're back! And you've been hit! Did you shoot him? Is he dead?" Bessy, still loud and dramatic, remained loud and dramatic.

"Shoot him?" I asked while smiling.

"Of course. No man hits a woman from the state of Alabama and lives without a bullet in his brain."

This time I laughed and it felt really good. "No, I decided against murder."

Bessy frowned. "I'd've shot his ass."

"Bessy Marie! That mouth!" momma scolded, though I was glad to hear it.

"Give me a hug," I told her, wrapping my arm around her shoulders. Bessy sank into me and I could tell that the feeling was mutual between we sisters. There was relief in her sigh and the way that she cuddled and such comfort cannot be explained.

"Sammy Jo!" That was Henry's little voice.

"He woke up," Bessy said, stepping back.

"Henry," I called and bent down to hug him as he ran waving his hands.

"Don't let him hurt your arm. Henry, please slow down." Momma was worried he'd slam into me and cause additional damage with his love.

"He's fine," I assured her, as he made his way to me, pausing when he noticed the brace on my arm and the bruising scattered on my face.

"You have boo boo's," he said. "Lots of 'em." His smile became a tiny frown.

"Yes, but I'm okay."

He reached and touched my face. His fingertips were gentle like a breeze. Tears stung my eyes, because he looked even taller, since I'd seen him before I left. I'd missed a month of his life and that made my heart ache when I thought about how he saw it. A month to Henry was the same as a year. What had he learned in my absence? Would he remember when he learned it I was gone?

"I missed you," I told him.

"I missed you," he replied and then kissed my swollen cheek.

"Let's get Sammy Jo inside. For thirty minutes you can ask her your questions. Then she's taking a nap. She needs some rest after all that travel."

We turned our heads in momma's direction and again I felt the joy of being home. I couldn't remember why I'd wanted to escape. Having my siblings around me, and my momma's strength, struck me as a priceless piece of wisdom.

"Did you bring us something?" Bessy asked.

I remembered the bag of gifts. I doubted those things had been put in my luggage. Did they even know where I placed them? They needed something from the world out there. I started to explain that I hadn't been able to bring everything back with me. Momma then said "in the seat. There's a box right there for the taking. That there box is what she brought home to you. Your sister mailed it before she left. You go ahead Bessy and carry it on in since that's the first thing you were concerned with."

I hadn't mailed anything home. I wasn't sure what was in that box or why momma thought it would be gifts. I didn't say anything in front of the kids. I hurried and sidled up to momma. "I didn't mail anything," I said, as quietly as I could speak.

"That woman said to look for it today and that was what it

was. I picked it up at the post office on my way to get you. It was there just like she said."

Gia. Again. Gia. I really needed to thank that lady, although it was Ezra that knew about the items. He told her to get them and send them. I wanted to personally thank him, see his face and hear his voice.

As we walked into the house Bessy put the box on the table and began opening it up. The kitchen table shook with her aggression. She was as excited about the contents as the younger two. I hoped everything was still inside. It wasn't much and the box was larger than needed. I figured Gia found the bag and stuffed everything in it so she didn't appear to be prying.

Bessy opened the flaps as Henry climbed in a chair so he could see inside. Hazel quietly watched as she lifted the bag and to my surprise the bag was stuffed.

"There's so much!" Bessy said with elation in her voice as she began to plunder the contents. She pulled out shirts and purses, hats and flashlights, with a map of the city laminated. There was a small toy replica of Grand Central Station and the Statue of Liberty in green. The jewelry, stuffed animals and bags of candy were from the M&M store in Times Square. I hadn't bought any of that. My budget would've exploded.

They squealed with delight as the three figured out what gift went to whom and why. I stood there watching unable to speak, smiling when they showed me with pleasure something that made them happy. Saying "you're welcome" to all their "thanks" seemed wrong for me to reply to. I hadn't done any of this. But I knew who did and I was humbled.

"What a fine thing to do," momma said.

My chest ached with the love before me. I was home. I was with my family. But I missed him. Ezra was vapor. Though here he was again in these gifts. He may be unreachable but my memories wouldn't permit me to forget him any time soon. I doubted they ever would. I had fallen in love with a man I couldn't have. Ezra was not to be "had." The man was smoke and that cloud had dissipated.

"You look surprised," momma said in a very low voice as she came to stand beside me.

"I only bought a fourth of that. I couldn't afford another dime."

Momma nodded. "The woman said Ezra was sending extra. Some things you mentioned the kids would like. Is Ezra the one who's got you in knots?"

Hearing someone say his name made it real. I needed that right now. To know he was real and that Ezra was actual, not the vapor or the smoke that he seemed.

"Yes," I replied. "He's the one."

Forty-Five

MOMMA WOULDN'T LET me go to work the next week. She said "rest and let your face heal. Then you can work with the public. They'll be nosey as is and we don't want to help that. They're already asking questions." Moulton was still small and Moulton remained Moulton.

Sleeping late and being alone in the house was something I'd never done. I've risen with the sun since I was old enough to walk and carry a basket. Momma had chores for all of us. This was odd. Being here alone.

Five days after my arrival I stood fixed before the coffee pot. The music of its brewing was enticing. Nine in the morning and the whole place was desolate and I thought to myself this is sad. I'm not a fan of this empty house. I wanted to go be with my family. See my friends without explanations. Jamie didn't know I was back yet. I hadn't told her because rehashing the story was a thing that really upset me. I couldn't have it both ways with bruises on my face so I quietly stayed in the house. She would eventually know the truth. Good or bad, Jamie got it all. But right now I wasn't ready to share that. My memories of Ezra were getting me through the day. I missed him more with each passing moment. I thought it was supposed to get easier, but my longing was getting worse.

The coffee finished brewing and I took a rare moment to appreciate the coffee maker. I'd missed having a regular no frills cup first thing in the morning when I woke up. The way the kitchen smelled from the coffee brewing and the memories that held made everything steady in my world.

I walked outside with my coffee into the warm summer morning. I'd never taken time to enjoy this place because I took it all for granted. I wouldn't do that again. Now I knew that every dream one might pursue didn't have the result they wished. Some were meant to be left alone, their silver linings really dark clouds.

"You look better." The male voice came from behind me and I jumped spilling my coffee. A small startled squeal shot from my throat, but it died instantaneously. I knew that voice. Knew that tone.

Spinning around, spilling even more coffee, I soaked in the sight of Ezra. He was here, in my backyard. Looking as beautiful and dangerous as ever, just like I remembered. The same as he was in last night's dream, but the dream was now reality.

"You're here," I blurted out, still in shock. I knew I was awake. The stinging on my hand from the burn of the liquid was my assurance this was happening.

He nodded and took several steps towards me. "I've been around."

"What? You've been around?"

He grinned and I melted just a smidge. "Yeah. Around. To make sure you were okay. Settled in."

Where exactly was "around" I thought? "What about your work for Hale?"

He shrugged and continued to look at me with that warmth in his stare that completed me and made my body feel whole again. Excited, he replied "that's handled. It will and can find its own end."

He was being evasive again. Weren't we beyond all of that? I would've thought the barriers and every single wall were now down. I took a step towards him and asked "who is Major? Tell me the truth."

The way his body tensed told me more than his mouth ever would. I knew this was something he never planned on sharing, though now it was exposed and bared.

"You were awake in the hospital." He didn't state it in the form of a question.

I nodded. "Yes I was."

With a sigh he ran his hand through his hair and then gave me the saddest smile. The kind that broke my heart and I didn't even know what he was going to say after that. "Major is the reason that we can't be," he replied with a motion between us. He pointed at me, and then himself. "I was born Major Colt. Then I decided to live my life in the shadows. Working a job that was full of excitement but is lonely. I don't think I realized how lonely until you. It's what I thought I wanted then I walked into Hale's and saw you for the very first time. I didn't expect to ever find . . . a you. Someone that would shatter me to walk away from."

There had to be an answer to this. Some solution to this. "But if you don't like your job just leave it."

He shook his head. "I can't. Major Colt is dead. I watched my own damn funeral. Saw my family and friends mourn me. It wasn't easy but I chose this life. Now I have to live what I chose. Ezra has no existence separate from work. If he wants it, well, if I want it, it can't happen because he isn't a person."

No, I wouldn't accept that. I wouldn't allow that excuse. "I love you," I told him without fear. Even if he didn't say the words to me I needed Major and Ezra to know. He was throwing "us" away. He had to think about that before he did it.

"You can't love a dead man," was his reply.

"Good thing you're not dead," I said.

He closed the distance and we embraced one another. The kiss I thought I'd never get to taste again was suddenly planted on my lips. Making my world contract. I was reminded that pieces of fairytales could happen, if only in slivers and sections, though you might not have them completely. Maybe your dreams couldn't be experienced, not as you completely dreamed them. You might simply and briefly touch them. Like tiny shards of a broken mirror. What was reflected was a piece of your longing. That gave you the permission to continue dreaming, knowing that hope was present.

I slid my hands up his arms and around his neck. My fingers played in the hair at his neckline. He moved down to my bottom to cup it and then drew me closer to his waist. I felt the arousal our kiss had caused. I'd never been this close to a man. I knew what I was feeling but the contours of his bulge was something I'd never touched. He ground into me and I reacted. My body hummed with want. This was what I'd been waiting for. Someone like Ezra to desire me. I wasn't going to let him go easily. I would fight until my very last breath.

When a hand slipped under my shirt my heart went wild in my chest. As it covered my breast I made a noise. It was similar to a moan, but it was more of a plea, for him to go all the way. For Ezra to take what he wanted.

He tugged my bra down and released my flesh into his eager rubbing grip. My breathing became erratic. I wasn't concerned with oxygen at the moment. I needed Ezra to fulfill this need. When he broke the kiss he muttered a curse under his heaving breath.

"Sammy Jo, I can't do this. Not knowing I have to leave."

Oh yes he could, because he would be back. He was afraid and didn't tell me he loved me, but I'd seen the look in his eyes, when I said the words to him. Ezra felt something or he wouldn't be with me in Moulton. He would've just walked away.

I then did all I knew to do. I pulled my shirt off, dropped it on the grass then discarded my bra the same way. When I reached for the buttons on my blue jean shorts Ezra grabbed my wrists. "Jesus, Sammy Jo," he groaned.

"We aren't stopping. This is happening." As soon as he let go of me I would finish undressing. I'd never been naked in front of a man. I could feel the blush creeping over my skin from the sheer exposure of my nudity. This would not keep me from what I wanted.

"Sammy Jo, I can't do this, knowing I'm not coming back."

"Yes you can," I replied. It was all I had to give him. I'd professed my love and that wasn't enough to make him stay with me. If this didn't work then at least I'd have the memory. "I want my first time to be with you."

He closed his eyes tightly and said "shit."

I patiently waited with his hand on my wrists. When he opened his eyes the look was new. There was heat, acceptance and desire. His hands left my wrists and went to my waist. "Let's go inside," he said.

The chill through my body interrupted my breathing. He had to grab me to keep me from falling.

Forty-Six

I WALKED INTO my house, topless, with Ezra's hands on my waist. The heat from his touch was like a bolt of lightning shooting through my body. We were barely inside when he moved me to the table and spun me around to face him, jerking me up against his chest before wildly kissing me again. I released my inhibitions. This would be my final chance. The last time I had Ezra completely to myself and I had to convince him to stay, that his life was solely with me. If it didn't this was all I would have and I wanted that perfect moment.

I tugged on the hem of his shirt. He tore it off and came back to me. My nipples stung with pleasure as they brushed against his chest. The muscles I'd only glimpsed, there against me impressively moving, the flex of his body and uncontained passion writhing and pulling me in. He kneaded my flesh and opened me up and I accepted whatever he did. Nothing had ever felt this amazing and I knew it never would. This would set the sexual bar for me and I knew no other could attain it. Still though, I didn't care. I was tired of caring. I wanted to get lost. To wander through the soul of this man.

Ezra's hands went down to my shorts. Without breaking the kiss he had them unbuttoned and sliding down my legs. Within seconds they were at my ankles. My mind wanted to shy away but I wasn't going to let it. This was my first. I wouldn't ruin it.

I stepped from my shorts when they hit the floor. He'd left my panties on. I wondered which pair I was wearing. I couldn't remember. When his hands went to cover my bottom he slid them under the fabric. Whichever pair they were would be fine with me because they wouldn't be on me for long.

"Sit on the table," he said, his voice thick and deep. I wasn't sure why I needed to sit on the table, but my knees felt weak so I figured that was a good idea. He didn't wait for me to do it. Making quick work of my panties he sat me on the table himself.

"I know you're a virgin Sammy Jo. But have you ever had your pussy eaten?"

I shuddered after the question. My body blushed from self-conscious embarrassment. I shook my head no and dropped my gaze. I'd never heard a guy refer to my vagina as a "pussy," with or without the word "eaten." I'd heard guys at school say the word before, but they weren't making reference to mine. Ezra was, and he was direct.

"Good," was his reply. He then knelt down in front of my legs, split them open and pulled them to him, settling them over his shoulders. Now I really wanted him to stop. This was more than I'd imagined when I thought about sex with Ezra and that was a lot.

Before I could make him quit his tongue touched me there. I almost bolted from the table. After two more seconds of this I wasn't going anywhere. Nor did I care that he was intimately involved in interviewing my vagina. I wanted him to stay where he was for as long as he chose to be there. It seemed to me this was a great idea.

My noises sounded like I was begging for more or I assumed that's what they meant. I couldn't be sure in my head. The pleasure was almost too much. I couldn't think clearly or focus on reason, because I didn't want to do either. My body was clawing for release, one that I was familiar with, because my fingers had brought me to climax many times.

However, this was more intense. It was stronger with a different pattern. My body was shaking with anticipation, or was it need or even desire? I wasn't positive, but I knew that when it broke it would crash like waves on a beach. If I could worry, my worry would be, that I might not survive the explosion. Though this seemed a good way to die.

With the ignition of the fireworks thinking wasn't useful, or if it was, I couldn't do it. I was thrown into another world, where nothing mattered but the bliss that controlled me. When I finally landed back on earth and my mind connected with my body, Ezra was naked before me. I was lightly being pulled into his arms, and then he spoke and said "Sammy Jo, where's your bed?"

My bed? Oh, where I sleep. I must've looked confused because a satisfied smile touched his face and he looked pleased, with himself and his deadly mouth. "It's your first time. We need a bed. Where is yours?"

Oh! Now it was time for the sex. In the bed that I shared with my sister? I wasn't sure about that. "What about the sofa?" I asked.

He cocked an eyebrow as if that were ridiculous. "Why not your bed sweetheart?"

He'd just been kissing between my legs. There was no reason to keep any secrets. Modesty has been thrown from the window: "I share it with Hazel, my sister."

A grin broke across his face and he chuckled: "so we can't have sex where your sister sleeps?"

I wasn't sure. Could we do that? "I don't know," I honestly replied.

Ezra sighed, his forehead resting against mine and this was his patient reply: "I think your sister will never know. So it'll be fine. I simply want you to be comfortable. Being your very first time."

He was right. I was being silly. "Okay. Sounds good to me."

With that response he chuckled and picked me up. "Point me in the right direction. I assume if we had this much of a struggle with deciding on the bed that you share, your mother's is completely off limits?"

I tipped my head with several quick jerks. "No way are we going in there."

That made him laugh and then I joined him.

"The room to the left is ours."

He carried me like I was a damsel, being rescued from a fire or something. I wanted to and had to say it: "what we did in there," I began, then paused, and he was immediately understanding.

"Yes? Go ahead and ask it."

My goofiness had to cease. I was almost nineteen years old. "That was oral sex." It was a question, but I didn't phrase it that way.

"That was me eating your pussy," he said. Then he rested me on my bed. His body hovered above me before he lowered himself against me and my mouth was open. All other thoughts then vanished. Ezra was skin to skin. The heat from our bodies increased. His pressing hardness was terrifying, though I wanted it to be inside me. I was ready. More than ready.

His knee opened my legs as I held his arms. I watched his face and his shifting body. I'd commit this scene to memory. When he was gone I would have this forever. I needed to remember it all.

"This hurts. You know that right?" He asked and his voice

sounded constrained like he was having difficulty controlling himself.

"Yes." I knew about the pain. My mother had scared us with it when she told us about sex and children. Although I doubted it actually felt like my insides were "being ripped open." Those were the words she chose. If it had been so bad for her the first time then why did she keep on doing it, spitting out babies left and right and acting like we couldn't hear them? That was a question that I never asked and the reason I didn't believe her.

Ezra bent his head and kissed my cheek, his breath warm against my skin. "I'll be easy," he promised and smiled.

Even if she was right I wanted the pain with him.

Forty-Seven

*I*T DID HURT. But I didn't care. As soon as Ezra was completely inside me he stopped and waited while peppering my face with kisses as if to soothe me. I lifted my hips to take him deeper once the initial stabbing and the wince that came with it were gone and my body adjusted.

"Are you okay?" he asked.

"Yes," my voice was raspy. I held onto his arms tighter waiting for him to move.

He took my encouragement, slid his hips closer before pulling away just enough, to ease it back in again. I knew this was how it was done, the mechanics of the thing, but the actual experience was beautiful. We were one. No Major or a secret life. There was nothing keeping us apart. He was altering my life forever. Ezra had become my "first."

"God, you're so fucking tight. It's taking all my will power not to lose control and bury myself deep inside you."

I wanted that. This was my chance to have all that Ezra could give me. If he was holding back I didn't want him to. "Show me, please, do it."

He paused and inhaled a shaky breath. "I can't. You're tender. It will hurt."

Yes he could. I wasn't missing this. If we never had this again I wanted every memory that was possible. "I'm begging you Ezra. Please. Go as deep as you can go. I want to be filled with you."

He tensed and bent his head to kiss me. I leaned into him arching my body. I could not have enough. I longed for his very last inch.

"Will you call me Major? While we're like this? I want to be who I am."

I nodded. He was Ezra to me, but I wanted to know him as Major. The man he was before. Had he been different when he carried that name? What had sent him running into a life in the shadows never to return again?

"Raise your knees. Tuck them near my waist."

I did as he said and I felt him go deeper. He was right, it hurt, but I still loved the feeling and wanted as much as he could give. Almost as much as I needed him to tell me he loved me while we were like this. As close as we could be. But he didn't, the words weren't his. Neither Ezra nor Major spoke of love.

He rocked his hips and brought us both to a climax. I shouted his name, his first, the name he wanted to hear. The name I wanted to know. Tears burned my eyes as he rolled to his side and took me with him for a warm embrace. Still close. Snug against his chest. This could be it and I knew that. This moment could be all I'd get.

Or it could be enough to make him stay.

We lay there in silence with our labored breathing slowing with each second that passed. I didn't want to move. I was afraid to break the silence. So I kept my thoughts to myself. Not asking him for more. Not telling him, yet again, that I loved him, so I said nothing.

Minutes turned into an hour before Ezra finally spoke. He'd kissed my head, his hands caressing my arm, while we were there lost in our thoughts. We weren't sure of the future before us. At least I wasn't, not knowing what he'd do.

"I'll never forget this," he finally said and my heart shattered into pieces. Those four words were what I needed to hear, everything I'd waited for. He wouldn't be staying. This hadn't been enough. Ezra was going to leave.

"Me either," was all I could say. It was too painful to speak. The urge to beg him was there, under the surface, the barely controllable crust of a wall I was attempting to currently maintain.

He kissed my lips, a peck, nothing more. "I can't tell you I love you Sammy Jo."

At least he was honest. I nodded. Any remnants of my heart were now gone. They combusted and evaporated. I was hollow, empty and broken, beyond any repair or fix.

"If I were still Major I wouldn't leave you. I would give you the life you want. The one that you hold in your dreams. The life I want more than I can tell you."

Again, I had no words. Couldn't even nod any more.

"My world isn't safe. I need to know that you're safe. Tell me you really understand."

I did. I wasn't enough. He had a life of excitement to chase and I wasn't enough to make him stay. He had excuses but I knew the truth. He didn't love me. That was the answer.

"You never promised me more," I managed to say. Anything else was a lie, and I wasn't a liar so I said it, but didn't feel better when I did.

Sighing wearily he laid his head on my shoulder, like the world was on his back. Ezra knew he'd broken my heart, and it was hard on him to react. Even though I tried to remain calm and let him go without shedding a tear, so that he wouldn't remember he'd crushed me.

"I can't come back," he said against my skin. "But I'll dream of you every night. My thoughts will always be wherever you are and I'll sense that you are with me. From now on I will never be alone. This is the memory I'll cherish. The one we're sharing right now."

That was too much. I needed him to stop if I was going to hold myself together. He was expecting a response, which was impossible.

We then separated, his body from mine, Ezra covering me with a blanket. He stood naked staring down at me. What strength I had met his gaze there above me, and this would be the last that I saw of him. The sorrow in his eyes mirrored what I felt, or maybe that was my imagination. Begging for this man to feel what I felt as he watched and said the expected: "goodbye Sammy Jo," he whispered.

I wouldn't say it, couldn't say it back. Instead I closed my eyes to block out the image of Ezra leaving the room. My memories would end in this bed. They wouldn't be permitted elsewhere.

His footsteps moved away from me. I listened as he dressed in the kitchen where he'd removed his clothing and mine. I waited in the hopes he'd change his mind and come back to me in the bed. If I stood up and went to him I knew I would cry and beg. I would, so I stayed put. Would he decide in there, with me in here, that we were worth fighting for? Enough for his own rebirth, as the man he'd been before Ezra?

He never came back. Neither Ezra nor Major. Both were gone in that instant. For hours I lay, long after his car drove away and the world was silent. The life was sucked from me. My soul seemed gone, my being vacated and nothing remained but pain. I was empty. He'd walked away. Just like he said he would. Just like

I'd hoped he wouldn't. One thing I knew for certain was that Ezra and this other called Major Colt weren't men who'd lied to me. They'd both been brutally honest. I had chosen not to believe them.

Epilogue

WILLIAMS HAD TO drive Hale north to White Plains to meet the cartel and get his coke. He had cash for the kilo and this deal was new and his connection was solid and reliable. He'd move the cocaine through his regular channels and then see if the purity was approved. His customers would let him know, though he kept barriers between them and himself.

As far as Williams knew they were going to meet a partner, a new guy that Hale had hired. He owned two restaurants around White Plains and though this was not unusual, it was early for Hale. They'd left New York at three in the morning with the snow and the ice cascading, falling in chunks and freezing the roads, though Williams knew what he was doing. Before he worked as a driver for Hale, this Williams had other employers. This Williams had been around.

"Sir, I'm sorry to bother you. It's this rest stop? The one on the right?"

"Yes Williams, just park underneath the floodlight, they will be waiting in a car like this one and will flash their lights when they see us."

"Very good. Thank you sir."

Hale didn't respond. Hale didn't say anything.

They exited slowly and cautiously from the road to the rest stop and Williams took his time. He dodged piled up ice with snow on its top and Hale didn't seemed bothered. The car he had mentioned was waiting. He was fifteen minutes early, so they must've been twenty and that didn't make him suspicious. This cartel was run by business men much like himself and his father, though his father didn't have what it took, so he remained in "legitimate business," while Hale expanded into dope and the cash that flowed with its selling.

"They are here," Williams said.

"Park fifty feet away so I can see them walk to me and then I'll need you to go wait in the restrooms. Here's a thousand for your inconvenience."

"Thank you sir. Such is appreciated."

Hale fisted the cash over the seat and Williams received it with a smile, looking over his shoulder one more time at his boss scowling from the back. As usual, he was proud of himself.

Williams parked and asked "is there anything else?" and Hale replied "do what I told you!" and Williams then said "so be it." He stepped from the car into the snow and when he closed the door they locked. Hale thought nothing of it, until no one exited the other black vehicle and he realized he was a hundred feet away and not the fifty he'd recently said.

"Williams! Get the fuck back in here and move us closer to them!"

Williams had simply and wholly evaporated into the ice and the snow and the gloom. Hale yanked at the door and it would not open and then he tried all the others unsuccessfully. When Ezra, Gia and Williams in a pack walked in front of Hale's idling car, they all stopped in the headlights and waved. Another vehicle then exited and picked the three up and they departed continuing north. Ezra, Williams and the driver didn't look, but Gia glanced over the seat, both cars exploding in a mushrooming blast and when she spoke she spoke to herself.

"I hate a motherfucker that beats on a woman."

Ezra replied "amen."

ABBI GLINES

ABBI GLINES IS a #1 New York Times, USA Today, and Wall Street Journal bestselling author of the Rosemary Beach, Sea Breeze, Vincent Boys, Existence, and The Field Party Series . She never cooks unless baking during the Christmas holiday counts. She believes in ghosts and has a habit of asking people if their house is haunted before she goes in it. She drinks afternoon tea because she wants to be British but alas she was born in Alabama. When asked how many books she has written she has to stop and count on her fingers. When she's not locked away writing, she is reading, shopping (major shoe and purse addiction), sneaking off to the movies alone, and listening to the drama in her teenagers lives while making mental notes on the good stuff to use later. Don't judge.

You can connect with Abbi online in several different ways. She uses social media to procrastinate.

www.abbiglines.com
www.facebook.com/abbiglinesauthor
twitter.com/AbbiGlines
www.instagram.com/abbiglines
www.pinterest.com/abbiglines

other titles by

ABBI GLINES

ROSEMARY BEACH SERIES

Fallen Too Far

Never Too Far

Forever Too Far

Rush Too Far

Twisted Perfection

Simple Perfection

Take A Chance

One More Chance

You We're Mine

Kiro's Emily

When I'm Gone

When You're Back

The Best Goodbye

Up In Flames

SEA BREEZE SERIES

Breathe

Because of Low

While It Lasts

Just For Now

Sometimes It Lasts

Misbehaving

Bad For You

Hold On Tight

Until The End

SEA BREEZE MEETS ROSEMARY BEACH
Like A Memory

THE FIELD PARTY SERIES
Until Friday Night
Under the Lights
After the Game (Coming August 22, 2017)

ONCE SHE DREAMED
Once She Dreamed (Part 1)
Once She Dreamed (Part 2)

THE VINCENT BOYS SERIES
The Vincent Boys
The Vincent Brothers

EXISTENCE TRILOGY
Existence (Book 1)
Predestined (Book 2)
Leif (Book 2.5)
Ceaseless (Book 3)

Made in the USA
San Bernardino, CA
04 December 2019